"The choice is yours tonight."

Dark velvet was in his words. "Just remember that I will hold you to your decision, even if you choose to take the risk."

"What risk?"

"The risk of inviting me into your bed."

Hearing it spelled out so bluntly sent a tremor through her. "What is the risk, Ryder? That you won't stay long in my bed?" She provoked him deliberately, ignoring the pain of that possibility.

His mouth crooked, and he lifted his fingers to spear them through the sleek knot of her hair, dislodging the clip. "The risk you're taking is that I *will* stay. Don't you understand, Brenna? I won't let you go after I've made you mine!"

STEPHANIE JAMES

is a pseudonym for best-selling, award-winning author **Jayne Ann Krentz**. Under various pseudonyms—including Jayne Castle and Amanda Quick—Ms Krentz has over 22 million copies of her books in print. Her fans admire her versatility as she switches between historical, contemporary and futuristic romances. She attributes a 'lifelong addiction to romantic daydreaming' as the chief influence on her writing. With her husband, Frank, she currently resides in the Pacific Northwest.

Stephanie James

AFFAIR OF HONOUR

™ SILHOUETTE®

*First published in Great Britain 2001
Silhouette Books, Eton House, 18-24 Paradise Road,
Richmond, Surrey TW9 1SR*

© Jayne Ann Krentz 1983

ISBN 0 373 80672 8

104-0101

*Printed and bound in Spain
by Litografia Rosés S.A., Barcelona*

STEPHANIE JAMES
COLLECTOR'S EDITION

Silhouette Books® are delighted to have the opportunity to present this selection of favourite titles from Stephanie James, one of the world's most popular romance writers. We hope that you will enjoy and treasure these attractive Collector's Edition volumes and that they'll earn themselves a permanent position on your bookshelves.

For Edna and Louis—Edna because she always reads each book and says nice things, and Louis because he always says nice things even though he doesn't read the books. And because I love them both.

One

"Don't stop now. This is just getting interesting."

The voice out of the darkness was as cool and deadly as the sound of a revolver being cocked. It has precisely the same effect on Brenna Llewellyn. She froze, one leg already swung over the sill of the window. She was trapped.

Fear-induced adrenaline surged into her bloodstream as she stared, wide-eyed, into the thick shadows of the bedroom she had been attempting to enter through the open window.

The price of a little impetuosity, she thought with fleeting hysteria. *My life.* Even as the words floated through her brain she was making the decision to flee. In such a situation there was little to lose. She had apparently surprised a thief or perhaps someone who had been using the deserted Lake Tahoe cabin as a hideout. Someone who would not particularly want any witnesses.

"No, I wouldn't try it if I were you," drawled the dangerous, darkly timbred masculine voice. "It's too late to change your mind."

Brenna's fingers clenched on the windowsill, knowing he was right. She was an easy target outlined against the moonlit sky behind her. By the time she could scramble back outside, the man concealed in the bedroom's shadows would be able to get off a shot. Assuming he was armed, of course, which was a perfectly reasonable assumption given the circumstances. Knuckles whitening under the strain, Brenna sat very still, straddling the window frame. She had to think. Panic would only hasten a disastrous ending.

"Look," she tried in a taut but amazingly quiet tone, "I haven't seen your face yet. There's no way I can identify you. Just let me go back the way I came and I give you my word of honor I won't tell a soul you're here."

"Your word of honor," mused the deep voice. Brenna winced at the amused sarcasm. "An interesting concept for a cat burglar."

There was a subtle flicker in the depths of the shadows, and Brenna caught her breath with sharp fear as her captor moved into a shaft of moonlight. "No, please…!"

It was too late. The silver beams streaming in the window behind her fell across the man who had halted her with his voice. Brenna swallowed tightly, her heart pounding with fear and the effort to control it. He was barefoot and naked above the waist, wearing only a pair of close-fitting black denim jeans. As he moved into view he lowered the weapon in his hands with a frighteningly casual motion that spoke of his utter familiarity with it. It was a bow and arrow.

Brenna, who had been preparing herself for the sight of a gun in his fist, was momentarily stunned by the unexpectedness of the primitive weapon.

"My God," she breathed. What had she stumbled into tonight?

"You might as well come all the way inside," the man ordered in a gentle voice that didn't fool Brenna for an instant. "You can't straddle that particular fence forever."

"Please, this is all a mistake…"

"I'll bet it is," he murmured, coming toward her with a deliberate, gliding movement that covered the distance between them much too quickly. "Life has a nasty way of making sure we pay for our mistakes. Haven't you learned that lesson yet in your profession of cat burglary?"

He reached out, setting aside the curving bow and the wicked-looking arrow without once taking his eyes off his victim. If she was ever going to have a chance, Brenna thought wildly, this was undoubtedly it.

With a frantic rush of tensed muscles, she twisted, trying to throw herself back out the window. But it was too late. A hand that felt like a manacle closed around her wrist and she was abruptly yanked over the sill and into the dark bedroom. Even as she stumbled and barely found her balance the man extended his free hand and flipped on the light switch.

Damn it, she wasn't going to give up without a fight, Brenna decided fiercely as her eyes locked with a pair of unbelievably cool gray ones. Something about the icy silver in that gaze fed the instinctive response of her body as she swung her foot in an arching kick and simultaneously went for his face with her nails. The cool silver told her this man was at home with the prospect of violence.

And in the next tempestuous moments, that gave him a distinct advantage. Before she had time to assimilate what had happened, Brenna found herself flat on her back, lying on a braided rug that had done little to cushion the impact of her fall. She was anchored beneath the unrelenting weight of a lean, masculine body that held her with ease. Shutting her eyes reflexively, Brenna gasped for the breath that had been partially knocked out of her.

"Damn you," she managed to hiss defiantly as he calmly caught her wrists in one of his fists and pinned them over her head. Then he knelt across her hips, a leg on either side of her body, and smoothly, efficiently began to run one hand over her.

Panic of another sort flared to life, and Brenna's body went rigid beneath his touch. "I swear to God if you rape me I'll see you hunted to the ends of the earth," she vowed, fury battling with fear.

"Relax," he growled. "I'm just trying to find out how lady cats are equipping themselves on the job these days."

Brenna stared up at him, confused. Then, through the haze of her terror, she realized that the touch of his hand was brisk and entirely impersonal as it moved across her red cotton knit pullover and jeans. Belatedly it dawned on her that he was searching for concealed weapons.

"I'm...I'm not armed," she managed, having to pause once in the middle of the short sentence in order to moisten her dry lips. "For God's sake, I'm not a burglar!" Instantly she regretted that confession. If he were a criminal hiding out here in the cabin, perhaps he would be more inclined to treat her leniently if he thought she was also on the wrong side of the law.

"Could have fooled me," he announced almost cheerfully, completing his search of her slender form and releasing her wrists. He continued to kneel astride her hips as he straightened and began to eye his captive in more detail. "Most of the people I've met who make a habit of crawling in through other folks' windows in the middle of the night have what are usually termed larcenous tendencies."

"Then you must hang out with a slightly different crowd than the one I run around with! I was not crawling through someone else's window," she added caustically, finding a heretofore undiscovered sense of nerve. "I was crawling through my own!"

One tawny brow lifted quellingly above one silvery eye. "I'm sure you've heard the old saying that possession is nine-tenths of the law. And as I happen to be in possession of these premises at the moment..." He let the sentence trail off meaningfully, waiting for her reaction.

"Illegally in possession!" she reminded him, more of her courage returning as she sensed some of the danger seeping out of the situation. She didn't know why her instincts told her things were looking more hopeful. After all, he was still pinning her to the rug, and the way he'd aimed that arrow at her earlier would probably give her nightmares for months. But there was a sort of calm *professionalism* about the man that made her think she wasn't dealing with an outright lunatic. At least he didn't appear to be the sort who was going to panic and kill her out of hand. That last thought reinforced her budding hope.

Looking down at her, he shook his head once in mock wonderment. "Illegally in possession," he repeated. "Imagine the world having come to the point where thieves in the night use phrases like that."

"Are you denying it?" she charged tightly.

"Oh, yes, I'm denying it. Want to see my lease?"

Brenna's amber eyes went very wide as she absorbed the implications of that casually dropped bombshell. "Your lease!"

"For three months beginning two weeks ago on the first of June," he told her easily, rising lithely to his feet and reaching down to grasp her wrist.

If there is a trauma as severe as facing danger, it is the horror of having thoroughly embarrassed oneself, Brenna reflected. In a very painful silence she allowed him to pull her to her feet.

"I think," she finally began very carefully, "there may have been some mistake."

"As I mentioned earlier," he drawled softly, watching her tense face, "mistakes tend to be paid for, one way or another."

Mutely she stared up at him, yanking her chaotic thoughts back into line with an effort of will. Surely she couldn't have clambered through the wrong window! But all the evidence was beginning to point to that, she realized grimly as she tore her gaze away from the silver-eyed man and hastily scanned the very lived-in looking bedroom.

The rumpled bed in which he had apparently been sleeping was a tumble of white sheets and patchwork quilt. The closet door stood open, revealing a collection of clothing that could only have belonged to a man. On the floor stood a pair of expensive-looking leather boots in an Italian design and a couple of pairs of casual shoes. Papers, books, and some magazine filled a small bookcase in one corner.

Brenna drew a long breath as she jerked her gaze away from the interior of the rustically designed bedroom and back to the man who was claiming possession. He was waiting, mouth smiling faintly at the corners as he watched the expressions flit across her features.

As she met his eyes once more, it struck Brenna that the faint edging of amusement around his hard mouth was enormously reassuring. This was not a man who would smile while still contemplating violence. She had the distinct impression that he could be ruthless and she'd had ample evidence that he could be dangerous when provoked, but he wasn't a nut, in spite of that bow and arrow sitting across the room.

Her nerves began to settle down and she raked an assessing glance over the man in front of her. He was about half a foot taller than she was, which made him nearly six feet. A rough estimate of the lines of experience that bracketed his hard mouth and narrowed gray eyes made Brenna think he was somewhere in his late thirties, perhaps thirty-seven or thirty-eight.

There was a sprinkling of silver at the temples of the tawny brown hair, which confirmed her age estimate. The hair itself was thick, cut a little too short for her taste, and was, at the moment, rather rakishly tousled. Only to be expected, she thought wryly, given the fact that she had clearly just gotten him out of bed.

There was nothing particularly handsome about the strong contours of his face, but the innate self-reliance and authority stamped there were oddly compelling. The silvery eyes were edged by lashes a shade or two darker than his hair. There was a hawk-like quality to the forceful nose and a rough-hewn look to the aggressive chin and the taut line of his high cheekbones.

Against her will, Brenna found herself aware of the expanse of smoothly muscled, bronzed male chest with its covering of curling tawny hairs. The low-riding black denim jeans sheathed a lean, boldly masculine frame that promised strength and grace.

For some reason she remembered how he had looked stepping into the moonlight, the bow and arrow in his strong, thoroughly competent hands. Calm, in command of himself and the situation; a true professional in the ultimate sense of the word. She had no idea what, exactly, he was professional *at*, but it was a cinch he would have been totally out of place at one of the college faculty meetings she was obliged to attend during the academic year.

She knew she was getting the same scrutiny in return and endured it with a sort of wry disdain. The bittersweet-chocolate-colored hair that fell to the middle of her back had come free of the clip at the nape of her neck and hung now in tangled disarray. It framed a face that had been alternately described as interesting and appealing but never beautiful. Wide, faintly slanted eyes of an amber-brown shade reflected intelligence and knew how to laugh when the occasion warranted laughter. A mouth that smiled easily was counterbalanced by the firm angles of her nose and jaw.

The red cotton knit pullover fit sleekly down over her slender body, clinging a little too closely to the small, unconfined breasts. Brenna shifted with a self-consciousness that annoyed her as she recalled the fact that she had dressed for the drive to Tahoe on the assumption that she would not be seeing anyone. Her jeans were snug and faded from numerous washings, and the moccasins on her feet were worn and comfortable.

At the age of twenty-nine, she ought to show more self-confidence in a trying situation, Brenna told herself. After all, she was now a faculty member of the philosophy department at a small but respected college. But she didn't feel particularly self-confident tonight. It had been a trying week in general, and this evening's fiasco was a fitting end to it.

"I'm sorry about this," she began with an attempt at decisiveness. "I appear to have crawled in through the wrong window." She lifted her chin at his mocking speculation. "I have a lease, too," she pointed out coolly. "It's the owner's fault for having booked two of us into the same cabin for the summer!"

"The owners are friends of mine. I don't think they would have made an error of that magnitude.

May I see your lease?'' He held out a hand prompt-
ingly.

"It's in the car," she hedged, frowning.

"Fine. Let's go and get it, shall we?"

"There's no need to be so rude about it!" Brenna
gritted as he took hold of her arm and led her out of
the bedroom and down the hall to the living room of
the cabin.

"I thought I was being remarkably patient," he
noted, opening the front door and propelling her
firmly out onto the porch.

Brenna had a brief mental image of what the grav-
eled drive was going to do to his bare feet and found
herself leading the way to the cream-colored Fiat
with alacrity.

He made no complaint, however, following her
with a long, pacing stride that was utterly silent and
catlike. He seemed oblivious to the rough gravel un-
derfoot. When they reached the car, he leaned casually on the low roofline and waited while she
opened the door and scrambled around in the front
seat.

"Here it is," Brenna announced with a note of
triumph she couldn't quite conceal as she found the
folder that contained the papers.

Wordlessly he took them and bent forward slightly
to read them in the pale light of the car's interior
bulb. "You're Brenna Llewellyn?"

"I can prove that, too!" she retorted tartly.

He smiled at that, straightening. "I'm Ryder
Sterne. Your neighbor for the summer, it would
seem."

"My neighbor!"

"You tried your breaking and entering techniques on the wrong cabin, I'm afraid. That's yours, the one over there behind mine." He waved a hand toward the woods behind the house Brenna had attempted to enter.

"I don't see...oh." Brenna stared into the darkened grove of pines, barely able to discern a structure in the shadows. "I never even noticed it," she confessed ruefully. "Damn it to hell. What a lousy way to conclude a lousy day," she added half under her breath. With an effort she made herself turn back to face the stranger standing beside her car.

"Do you always make it a practice to go in through windows?" he demanded almost pleasantly, silver eyes reflecting the moonlight.

"Don't be ridiculous," she told him stonily. "I tried the key and it didn't work. That's why I was using the window."

He nodded. "I heard you fiddling with the lock. If you'd waited I would have answered the door and saved us both a great deal of trouble. As it was, when I heard you leave the porch and start around to the back of the house, I was left to assume your intentions were less than honest."

"So you waited for me with a bow and arrow?" Brenna tossed back accusingly.

He shrugged, offering no apology. "It was the only weapon I had conveniently at hand. How did I know who or what was going to come through that window? Come on, let's get your things out of the car. It's two in the morning and I'd like to get some more sleep tonight!"

Alarmed, Brenna put her hand restrainingly on his

bare arm, withdrawing it almost at once as she became acutely conscious of the feel of sinewy muscles.

"That's all right, I can manage," she told him
imperiously. "I'm very sorry for the mix-up, but you
can feel free to go back to bed. I don't need any help
tonight."

He glanced down at his bare arm where she had
touched him briefly. When he looked up again, it was
with the faintest of smiles. "I'll carry your things
over to the cabin," he repeated very gently. "But I
think I'll put some shoes on first. Hang on, I'll be
right back."

Brenna watched him move back toward the house
with that effortless, silent stride, her mouth open in
astonishment. She was accustomed to men who
would have argued, perhaps, or backed off once their
offer had been rejected, or, in some instances, men
who might have tried to reason with her that she did
indeed need some help. She was not accustomed to
men who simply made gentle pronouncements and
then proceeded to carry them out over her expressed
wishes in the matter.

She was learning, she told herself laconically as
Ryder returned to the car and reached inside without
a word to lift out the luggage. The gentler the tone,
the more this man meant business. The memory of
how softly he had spoken when he'd ordered her not
to try escaping was still fresh.

Besides, she consoled herself as she picked up a
small case, it *was* two in the morning. At this hour
very little seemed worth arguing about.

"If you'll try that key on this lock, I think you'll

find it will work,'' Ryder instructed kindly, pausing on the front porch of the A-frame cabin Brenna had rented.

She slanted him a quelling glance as she dug out the key for the second time that night. ''I'll make a deal with you,'' she grumbled. ''Promise me you won't bring up tonight's little fiasco all summer long and I won't spread the word that you greet guests with a bow and arrow, okay?''

In the pale light she saw his mouth skew upward at the corner. ''You drive a hard bargain. I'll have to think about it.''

The charmingly rustic interior of the A-frame was revealed as Ryder found the light switch. Brenna glanced around interestedly. As promised, the cabin seemed fully equipped. A flight of stairs led from one side of the fireplace-dominated living room to a loft arrangement that served as the bedroom. The kitchen, dining, and living areas downstairs flowed comfortably together and appeared sufficiently furnished with large, low pieces of solid construction.

''Can you really see the lake from here?'' Brenna asked dubiously, peering out into the darkness through the floor-to-peaked-roof windows.

''You'll get a better view in the morning. Too many trees in the way tonight.'' Ryder set down his load. ''Come on. One more trip should do it.''

''A man of few words. The strong, silent type, I suppose,'' Brenna muttered behind him.

''Only at two in the morning,'' he retorted, not bothering to glance back over his shoulder.

Brenna, who was chewing her lip, was just as glad

he hadn't turned around to witness her reddening cheeks. What a dumb remark!

"I think, since we're both wide awake now," her new neighbor announced calmly a few minutes later as he lifted out the last suitcase, "that we both need a nightcap. Come on inside." Still holding the last bag, he started toward his own front door.

Brenna saw her property disappearing in the direction of his cabin and hurried to protest. "Thanks, that's very kind of you under the circumstances, but not necessary. I'm sure I'll sleep very well after all the excitement, and it's getting so late…"

"But I might not sleep well at all. Come in, Brenna Llewellyn," he commanded ever so softly, holding the door politely.

Brenna, not knowing what else to do, walked resentfully inside.

"Have a seat. I'll get a couple of glasses."

She watched, narrow-eyed, as Ryder moved into the kitchen with that gliding way he had, and the she turned around to glance automatically at the books lining a nearby shelf. Force of habit, she thought dryly. Always check out a stranger's bookshelf first. With a creature as enigmatic as Ryder Sterne, a person could use a few clues to his personality!

The array of paperbacks on the top shelf produced an ironic expression in Brenna's amber eyes as she reached up to pluck out a volume. Exactly what she should have expected, she decided, perusing the lurid cover, which portrayed a raffish male firing a wicked-looking gun at a cluster of obviously evil types who, in turn, seemed bent on murdering the hero and the sexy blonde clinging to his left biceps.

It was the sort of sleazy, category stuff usually labeled men's adventure fiction, Brenna told herself disdainfully, unaware of how her mouth had curved downward until Ryder's gentle voice came from across the room.

"That's not the worst of it, I'm afraid," he told her as if he'd just read her mind. "I not only read it; I wrote it."

"What?" Startled, Brenna glanced back at the paperback cover. "It says the author is Justin Murdock."

"A pseudonym." Ryder set down the two glasses of brandy he was carrying, making room for them among a clutter of archery texts on the old brassbound trunk that served as a coffee table. He sank smoothly into the depths of a couch that displayed a genteel shabbiness suitable for a mountain retreat and held out one of the snifters. "Here you go. Don't worry, it's good. I never let my heroes drink anything but the best.

"I'm impressed," Brenna drawled, accepting the bell-shaped glass and sipping obediently at the very excellent brandy. Cautiously she sat down across from him in a padded rattan chair.

"Impressed by the brandy or the books?" he asked pointedly.

"Both." Damned if she was going to let him put her on the defensive.

"But it's not exactly your kind of fiction, right?" He smiled.

"Not exactly. But who am I to argue with success? I take it you are rather successful at it?"

"Very."

"I see. Well, congratulations."

"And now that we know my line of work, it's your turn."

Brenna sighed, her lips tightening unconsciously as she met his steady gaze over the rim of the glass. "I'm an assistant professor of philosophy at a small college in the San Francisco Bay area."

He said nothing, but something akin to amusement flickered in the silvery eyes.

"You find my career humorous?" Brenna challenged in a tone as dangerously gentle as any he could have used. Damn it, she'd been through enough this past week concerning her career! She didn't have to hear it mocked on top of everything else!

"Your career seems a little at odds with the memory of that cat burglar who came crawling through my window half an hour ago!"

"There was a time, Mr. Sterne," she returned, lecturing with an acid sweetness, "when the philosopher was also expected to be a person of action!"

"But probably not illegal action. At any rate, you'll have to admit that in the modern era the majority of academic types live in the ivory towers of their institutions of higher learning and seldom emerge to face the real world. Unless you want to count those suitably dramatic moments when they sally forth to face the menace of television cameras in the name of a fashionably radical cause," he added reflectively and then shook his head. "No, I don't think you can count those moments. They hardly constitute reality."

Brenna arched a brow, refusing to be drawn. "It

would seem we are on opposite sides of an issue that has been around a long time. I doubt that we can settle the age-old hostility between those who promote the use of reason and those who admire the machismo approach to life. You, clearly, have made a nice living out of romanticizing the excitement of violent action. I, on the other hand, have just spent an entire semester trying to drum the concept of ethics into the heads of fifty freshmen.''

Which was surely some sort of joke, when you thought about it, Brenna added silently. Imagine having spent all that time teaching an ethics class only to discover one was the victim of the most unethical behavior...

But Ryder was looking more amused than ever. ''So we are opposing forces, hmmm? Haven't I heard something about opposing tensions ultimately producing harmony?''

Brenna blinked in astonishment, pausing in the act of raising her glass. ''Heraclitus.''

He looked blank. ''I beg your pardon?''

''Heraclitus,'' she repeated slowly. '' A sixth-century Greek philosopher who theorized that there was an underlying harmony in nature and that it was the product of opposing forces.'' In spite of herself a slow smile crept into her golden eyes. ''As I recall, he used the bow as an example of tension creating harmony.''

''A bow?'' Ryder suddenly looked intrigued. ''Yes, that makes sense. There is a perfect balance of tension involved in nocking an arrow and drawing the bowstring. I like the notion.'' He nodded decisively. ''I'll have to throw it into the book I'm starting next week.''

''Just like that?'' Brenna demanded. ''Wouldn't you want to study the fine points of the philosophy in a little more depth? Shouldn't you read the theory in more detail?''

''I doubt that would prove worth the effort.'' He shrugged. ''I'd only take what's useful, and it sounds like you just gave me the useful part. The main research I'm doing for the book is in the actual use of the bow and arrow as a commando weapon.''

She wanted to lecture him on the reprehensibleness of such slipshod research techniques, but Brenna found herself momentarily sidetracked. ''A modern commando weapon? The bow and arrow? Good grief! I thought that was left behind after the invention of gunpowder!''

''The bow and arrow was used as recently as Vietnam,'' Ryder told her, leaning back against the cushions and sipping his brandy. ''On a very limited basis, of course. Despite modern technology there still aren't very many ways of killing people quietly from a distance. The bow makes a very useful weapon in the hands of a man who must move silently in and out of an enemy-occupied zone on, say, a reconnaissance mission.''

Brenna stared at him and shuddered in disgust. ''I can see why you wouldn't want to burden your reader with the philosophical implications of a drawn bowstring. You are, after all, selling violence and action, not ethical philosophical theory!''

''And sex.''

She glared at him.

"I'm selling sex, too. It goes nicely with the violence and action," he explained politely.

"I'm sure it does." She'd had enough. Brenna got to her feet, determined to put a decisive end to a fruitless conversation. "Thank you very much for the brandy and the help in unpacking my car, Ryder. Now I think it's time I let you get back to bed." She was already striding briskly for the door. "You've been very patient, considering the way I woke you earlier," she admitted grudgingly.

"I'll see you back to your cabin." He was behind her yet he reached the door before she did. The man moved like fog, Brenna thought in annoyance. Silent, smooth, overtaking you before you knew it.

"That's really not necessary," she tried valiantly. "I can find my way."

"I'll see you to your door," he repeated.

She lifted one shoulder in silent resignation. He was using that gentle tone of voice again. Hardly any point in continuing the argument.

Neither said a word until they reached her front porch, and then something occurred to Brenna. Turning in the act of inserting her key into the lock, she peered up at her escort, studying the reflection of moonlight in his silvery eyes.

"What is it, Brenna?" he prompted indulgently.

"Did you really think I was a cat burglar when I first came through that window?"

His mouth curved upward but his dark voice was very serious. "The thought definitely went through my mind. I don't normally greet ladies with a bow and arrow. Why are you smiling?"

"No reason," she assured him hastily, stepping

over the threshold and swiveling to close the door. "No reason at all. Good night, Ryder."

He nodded once and moved off as softly as the moonlight itself.

Brenna hesitated a moment longer in the doorway, the faint smile he had questioned fading slowly. How could she possibly have explained the curious flicker of amused excitement she had felt at the thought of a man like Ryder actually mistaking her, of all people, for a cat burglar?

She was an academician, a student and teacher of philosophy. Not a woman of dangerous action! Slowly she closed the door and stood gazing unseeingly at the cozy interior of her summer home.

And furthermore, Ryder Sterne had been wrong when he proclaimed that her career provided some protection from the realities of life. Brenna's hands tightened on the doorknob before she made herself release it and walk slowly across the worn, flower-patterned rug in front of the fireplace. There was no protection, no escape from the decision that had been forced upon her this week.

Nor, she thought with a return of disappointment and anger, could she look for help from the one man who should have stood by her. Damon Fielding had made his position clear when he'd stopped by her apartment this morning to "reason" with her.

His advice had been thoroughly practical, thoroughly rational, and thoroughly shocking when one considered that it came from a full professor of philosophy and ethics. He had urged her to accept the situation as it was, not to fight back. Her career, after all, was at stake.

Certainly, he agreed, the action of the department head in publishing Brenna's research and analysis as his own was unethical, but that sort of thing happened all the time in the academic world. She must remember that Paul Humphrey was on the verge of retirement. She must also keep in mind the fact that Damon Fielding was widely thought to be the next in line to assume the mantle of head of the Department of Philosophy. If she would just keep quiet and not make any waves, the aging Dr. Humphrey would soon be out of the picture.

Wasn't it worth ignoring the injustice for the sake of her future career? Besides, Damon had pointed out with a practical logic that probably would have appealed to someone like Ryder, she couldn't hope to win in any open confrontation with Dr. Humphrey. She was only an assistant professor, too far down on the rung of the academic ladder to tackle the respected head of the department.

But all Damon's arguments had succeeded in doing was to put a very large question in Brenna's heretofore career-oriented mind. Did she truly want to continue in a profession that taught such concepts as the pursuit of truth and ethical analysis yet practiced the same kind of pragmatic politics found in the far less self-righteous world inhabited by people like Ryder Sterne?

It was a decision she had to make in the next few weeks.

Two

She might be at a turning point in her career and therefore in her life, Brenna told herself firmly the next morning, but she must not forget her responsibility to Craig. Her younger brother was also rapidly reaching some inner turning point. She could sense it, even though he did his best to appear content with his college studies. Just one more year, Brenna thought hopefully. One more year and he'll graduate. Then he can take some time to explore the various directions open to him. Just so he gets that degree!

It was going to be a decisive summer in more ways than one.

Brenna showered in the early morning chill of the cabin. Then she slipped into the jeans she had worn last night and dug out a white cotton pirate shirt from one of the suitcases. The full sleeves gathered into French cuffs, and the classic, slit-front collar made for a casually dashing look that appealed to her on that particular morning.

Standing in front of the mirror in her loft bedroom, she brushed her chocolate-colored hair straight back from her forehead and twisted it into a loose configuration at the back of her head. The severe style emphasized the slant of the amber eyes that stared back at her with such seriousness this morning. What was she going to do?

Wandering into the kitchen, she located a copper-bottomed teakettle and set it on the stove. A short rummage in the small sack of groceries she'd brought along produced the packet of tea. Brenna was reaching for one of the pottery mugs in a cupboard near the sink when she glanced out the window and saw Ryder.

The uneasy shock she had experienced at their first meeting returned in diluted form. This morning he presented no overt threat, but there was something about this man that suggested a poised menace to her senses. The peculiar sensation had not disappeared overnight.

He stood at the edge of the clearing near his cabin, aiming a bow and arrow at a target that had been tacked to a tree. The morning sunlight gleamed on the tawny hair and clearly outlined the lean, smoothly coordinated masculine figure. A quiver of arrows was buckled to his hip and a leather arm guard protected his wrist beneath the rolled-up sleeve of the yellow shirt he was wearing with his black denim jeans.

The bold stance and the harshly carved features suggested a man who knew and understood the rough side of life. In fact, Brenna decided wryly as she poured the boiling water into her mug, he looked as if he could have doubled for one of his own fictional heroes. All he lacked was the sexy blonde clinging for his biceps!

She looked up from pouring the tea water in time to see him loose the nocked arrow. It came as no surprise when the shaft thudded forcefully into the center of the target. In a smooth motion Ryder removed another arrow from the quiver, nocked it, and drew the bowstring. It found a place on the target very close to the first.

As if sensing her eyes upon him, Ryder glanced toward the kitchen window before reaching for a third arrow. Through the glass their eyes met, and then without a pause he started toward Brenna's cabin.

Reminding herself of her manners and the way she had behaved the previous night, Brenna met him at the door with a cup of tea.

"Thanks," he murmured, accepting it gratefully as he set down the bow and quiver on her kitchen table.

"Not as good as your brandy, perhaps, but drinkable." She smiled.

"I was wondering if you'd brought some food along for yourself. I was going to ask if you needed to cadge a meal off me this morning." He stood looking down at her, silver-gray eyes roving her scrubbed features.

"We philosophers are not so far removed from the plane of reality as to forget things like food!" She chuckled as he dropped into a straight-backed chair at the table and sipped his tea with appreciation.

"You don't look like a teacher of philosophy this morning," he said in a soft purr of a voice that brought Brenna's senses alert. "But, then, you didn't look like one last night, either."

"Appearances can be deceptive. One of the first rules of good philosophy," she informed him with a determined lightness.

"One of the first rules of any intelligent approach to life," he countered seriously. "Would you like to go out with me tomorrow night?"

Startled by the abrupt question following so quickly on the heels of a totally unrelated subject, Brenna stared at him, her lips slightly parted in surprise.

"To the Gardners'. They own these cabins, remember? They have a place of their own a few miles from here. I'm invited for dinner and I thought you might like to come along. I'm sure they would be pleased to meet you in person."

"Oh, Well, I see. That's very thoughtful of you, but—"

"Good." He nodded once. "We'll leave around six thirty."

"Mr. Sterne…Ryder," she amended quickly, her brow furled in irritation, "I was not accepting the invitation. I was thanking you for it and was about to decline, in fact. I have a great deal to do here and—"

"And you've got all summer to do it." Ryder grinned at her. It was the first time she'd witnessed that particular expression. She'd seen his rather serious smiles a few times, but this was an outright, thoroughly wicked masculine grin. It was captivating. "Besides, you owe me. I'm calling in the tab."

"I owe you! That's ridiculous. What for?"

"For the fright you gave me last night, naturally."

It took a second for Brenna to catch her breath. For some strange reason she wanted to stare and go on staring at the slashing grin. "You didn't look particularly frightened, as I recall!" she finally managed coolly.

The grin disappeared, changing back into one of the sardonic smiles. "A man learns to deal with it."

"Fear?"

"Ummm." He took a long swallow of his tea. Then he gave her a straight look. "And I wasn't the only one handling it fairly well last night."

"If that's some sort of macho compliment you're handing down condescendingly to the little lady, forget it!" Brenna wasn't quite sure why she was reacting so fiercely.

"There's nothing condescending about it," he told her very quietly. "Courage is an admirable trait in anyone." He held up a hand to ward off her rejoinder. "Wait, I'll rephrase that. Courage is something *I* admire in anyone, male or female. There, I'm not generalizing, I'm speaking only for myself. Okay?"

"I wasn't going to argue," Brenna said slowly. "I, too, happen to admire courage in others."

"Ah! A point of agreement, perhaps?" he teased.

"But I have the distinct impression," she continued calmly, "that the sort of courage you would appreciate is somewhat different from that which I would applaud."

"You think so?" he charged almost casually, watching her with interest.

She nodded thoughtfully. "For you courage would consist of a physical approach to danger. I tried to fight you last night and you find that commendable. From my point of view it was only desperation. I panicked and I reacted instinctively. It wasn't courage as you term it. Real courage is the kind shown by men and women who refuse to back down from the conviction of their ideas simply because the majority doesn't like those ideas. Or because someone in authority doesn't approve of those ideas. A brave man is one like Socrates who allowed himself to be tried and sentenced to death for his philosophic teachings even though he probably could have escaped. He respected the concept of law too much to defy it. Or the English humanist philosopher Sir Thomas More who defied Henry the Eighth by refusing to go along with Parliament trying to make the king head of the Church."

"More got himself executed, too, I take it?" Ryder inquired sardonically.

"Yes. He was found guilty of treason." In a way Damon had tried to convince her it was almost treason to challenge the head of the philosophy department, she reflected.

"Well, I'm not going to say they weren't men of courage and honor," Ryder announced judiciously. "Although I'm not particularly into martyrdom myself. That still doesn't make your bravery last night any less admirable. You knew you were outmatched from the start but you fought anyway. And went on defying me even after I'd pinned you down. That takes guts, lady.''

''Sounds more like stupidity to me,'' she found herself retorting on a note of sudden laughter. ''If I'd tried talking first, I might have got the whole misunderstanding straightened out before I found myself flat on my back being searched for concealed weapons! A clear instance of where reason should have prevailed.''

''Easy to say in retrospect,'' Ryder noted. ''At the time, though, you were forced to make a choice on a limited amount of evidence. There wasn't really an opportunity to try reason first and violence second. Sometimes choices like that are forced on us and we do the best we can in the circumstances. Besides, we each learned something about the other. Something it might have taken longer to learn otherwise.''

Brenna cocked a disbelieving eyebrow. ''What in the world did we learn?''

He must have caught the challenging note in her tone because a trace of the dashing grin flashed across his face. ''You found out I don't let rash little lady cat burglars climb through my window with impunity and that I don't resort to rape.'' He ignored the wave of red in her cheeks. ''I, on the other hand, learned you don't cower when the chips are down and that you feel good under my hands.''

''That I feel good!'' Brenna repeated furiously, remembering the way his hands had stroked her body looking for weapons. The red in her cheeks darkened in anger and embarrassment. She had thought his touch almost impersonal at the time. Clearly he remembered the search procedure well! ''It's hardly gentlemanly of you to remind me of the way you held me down and went through my pockets! In fact, it wasn't the thing to say at all if you're actually trying to ask me out for a date tomorrow night!''

''I'm counting on your remembering that I don't resort to rape.'' He smiled blandly. ''I proved myself unthreatening last night.''

''And that's supposed to be a sufficient reason for me to accept your invitation?'' she demanded, knowing she was half charmed and half incensed by his approach to the matter of getting a date.

''Don't you want to meet your landlords?'' he asked coaxingly.

''I don't see that it's necessary. I have strictly a business relationship with them.''

''They're nice people. And as I said, you owe me.''

''You have such a persuasive technique,'' she muttered dryly, knowing her sense of humor was going to get the better of her. Besides, she could certainly use the diversion of an evening out with a man who was totally different from Damon Fielding or anyone else on the philosophy faculty!

''Did you have anything better to do tomorrow night?''

''Not particularly,'' she admitted. ''Okay, I'll go with you to meet the Gardners if you're sure they won't mind your turning up with a stranger in tow.''

He finished his tea and got to his feet, looking satisfied. ''They won't. I called Sue Gardner first thing this morning and told her I was bringing you along.''

Brenna looked up at him, remaining firmly in her

chair. "Why do I have this feeling you don't lack self-confidence? Do you always organize and manipulate things so that they go the way you want them to go?"

"I've picked a way of life that allows me to live on my own terms," he told her quietly, holding her eyes.

A current passed between them, an electric tension that Brenna felt with overpowering awareness. The menace her senses responded to in him was back in full force.

"But I'm not part of your life," she heard herself say very clearly. It seemed important to tell him that. She wanted no misunderstandings on the issue. They were neighbors for the summer, nothing more. They were truly from two different worlds.

"Do you philosophy types routinely go around denying reality and the evidence of your own senses? You entered my life last night when you came through my window. This morning I can reach out and touch you…"

He lifted the hand with which he drew the bowstring and put it under her chin. The silvery eyes looked deeply into hers, trapping her momentarily in their glittering depths. "Oh, yes, Brenna Llewellyn. You're definitely part of my life."

"Only…only for the summer," she whispered hoarsely, wishing desperately that she could find the willpower to move away from him. What was she letting him do to her? Was she crazy?

He shrugged dismissingly. "That's long enough, I imagine."

Brenna saw the sudden intention in his gaze and

made a belated movement to escape. But she was much too slow. The hand under her chin reached around to anchor her gently by the nape of the neck. Bracing his left hand on the back of the chair on which she was sitting, Ryder leaned down to kiss her.

Summing up the situation immediately, Brenna held herself passively still. She sensed the curiosity in him, the exploratory approach. She was a woman he would be living next door to for several weeks and he was testing the waters. The logical response for her to make was polite, bland disinterest. A struggle might provoke a man like this who believed in action and force. So Brenna sat unmoving as his mouth came down on hers.

His lips were warm, firm and questioning. She had been right, she told herself. He was curious about her. She kept her eyes open although his own dark tawny lashes flickered against his cheeks when his mouth made contact. The fingers at the back of her neck moved with a massaging sensuality while his lips explored hers.

Brenna's fingers tightened on the edge of the table as she held herself stiff and unresponsive. There was more in this slow, questioning embrace than mere curiosity, she realized abruptly. There was a hunger lying in wait. It was held in check and it was, at the moment, unthreatening. In spite of her resolve, she found herself wondering what it would take to unleash it.

Ryder didn't pursue the kiss long. He brushed her lips one last time with his own and then lifted his head an inch or two and opened his eyes. There was a cloudy veil concealing the truth in the gray depths of his gaze, but there was a whimsical tilt to his mouth.

"No?" he asked very gently.

"No." Brenna's voice was very assured and she met his eyes in a straight look.

"Is there someone else?" He didn't move, retaining his hold on the nape of her neck.

Brenna drew in her breath. "Someone else; something else. A lot of reasons."

The tilt of his mouth widened into the rakish grin for an instant and the silvery eyes gleamed. "Reasons that vague I can handle," he told her with an amused arrogance.

Perhaps it was time to take a firmer stand. "I'm not here for a summer affair, Ryder."

He straightened. "Why are you here?"

"To work. To sort out some things in my life. To make some decisions."

"More vagueness. Does philosophy teach you to be vague in the face of a direct question?"

"Sometimes," she retorted, deliberately being vague again. But humor lightened her tone now.

"Amazing. No wonder they keep your sort locked up on college campuses. You'd flounder to death if you had to stay very long in the real world!"

"Your prejudice against the academic world is showing."

"Your prejudice against my world has already surfaced," he shot back dryly. "Come outside with me and let's see if we can find a common interest."

"How?" she asked.

"I'll teach you to use the bow. When you use it properly, you can think of it as an application and illustration of the philosophic principle of harmony in the universe.'' He chuckled, taking her hand and pulling her to her feet.

''While you'll be thinking of it as a lethal weapon for one of your heroes!''

''So? Just because it's your nature to look for something intellectually elevating in the exercise, don't condemn me for looking for something practical.''

''I wouldn't dream of condemning you for that!'' she scoffed, letting herself be led outdoors into the still-cool mountain morning. She glanced to her left, automatically taking in her surroundings en route to the archery target, and gave a sudden gasp of appreciation.

''Oh, you *can* see the lake from here! The rental agent was right. Isn't it fantastic? It's huge. Like an inland sea!''

The dazzling blue depths, so deep the lake never froze even in the heart of winter when the region was converted into a skiing wonderland, reflected the bright morning sun.

''It's about twenty-two miles long,'' Ryder told her. ''And about eight miles across at this point. Do you gamble?''

''I beg your pardon?'' she asked in surprise.

''I just wondered if you were interested in gambling, since you've elected to spend your summer on the Nevada side of the lake,'' he explained as they reached the point near the target where he had been standing earlier.

''Oh, I see what you mean. No, I'm not particularly interested. I saw the casinos as I drove through town last night,'' she added. ''I just happened to wind up here because this looked like the most attractive area available from the agent.''

''Fate,'' he suggested dramatically, loosing her hand to unstrap the leather arm guard from around his wrist.

Brenna chuckled. ''I'm afraid there is no empirical evidence to suggest that fate is a genuine factor in the world.''

''Lively conversation like that must limit your dating to other faculty members,'' he murmured, taking hold of her left wrist and attaching the guard. ''So I can assume the 'someone else' is another member of your philosophy department staff?''

''You do a pretty good job of lining up the evidence yourself,'' she commended casually, examining the wrist guard.

''He doesn't love you, you know,'' Ryder continued, bending down to pick up the quiver of arrows.

Brenna swallowed in a wave of uneasy anger. She should not let herself be drawn into this kind of conversation. ''That's your opinion!''

Her put the bow in her hand and looked into her eyes.

''That's another deduction from empirical evidence,'' he corrected.

''What evidence?'' she asked huskily.

''He let you come alone to Tahoe for the summer.''

''And from that you assume he doesn't love me?'' she challenged, amber eyes kindling.

''I'm a man. Given what I know about being a man, that's a reasonable assumption.''

"You're very sure of yourself," she taunted, vividly aware of his closeness and the confidence in which he was enveloping her.

"Want to hear another assumption?" he baited softly.

"I doubt it!"

"You don't really love him, either," he concluded inexorably.

"You'd like to believe that so you don't have to feel guilty when you make a pass at me," she tossed back, proud of the coolness in her voice as she studied the weapon in her hand. Why was she standing there, letting him goad her like this? She should drop the bow and walk back to the cabin and lock the door. But that would be admitting that she couldn't deal with him, wouldn't it?

"I won't feel guilty when I make a pass, don't fret." He laughed far back in his throat. "I don't feel even a pang about that kiss, for example."

"Why do you say I don't love him?" She couldn't resist the question, even though she was disgusted with herself for asking.

"Because you are a woman who concerns herself with such things as honor. If you were in love you would not risk conversations like this with another man," he told her simply. "Now," he went on before she could find an answer, "this is called a recurve bow. The way the ends curve and deflect back give a lot more leverage. You're right-handed so you stand with your left side toward the target. We'll start with an open stance…"

He knelt in front of her and guided her sandaled feet into the appropriate positions. Brenna found herself listening submissively for a while as he directed the placement of her hands, talked about the basics of safety, and generally involved her more and more deeply in the first lesson. He was good, she realized. An excellent teacher, in fact. If there was one thing she could admire other than sound scholarship, it was the ability to teach.

"My God! It's hard," she suddenly complained in astonishment when the time came to practice drawing back the bowstring. "I'll never be able to draw it far enough to nock an arrow!"

"Sure you will. This is considered a very lightweight bow. A strong woman like you can handle it."

"What makes you think I'm strong?" she protested, taking a deep breath and attempting once more to draw the bowstring.

"I was the one holding you down on the floor last night, remember?" he said, grinning.

"I thought we agreed you wouldn't bring that up again," she muttered caustically.

"I agreed to think about the bargain you suggested. I haven't made up my mind to accept it yet. There, that's it. I told you that you could do it."

She slackened the tension on the bow so it wouldn't snap and threw him a glare. But she said nothing else as he took her through the basic fundamentals of archery.

"These are aluminum-shafted arrows," he told her as he handed the first one to her. "The best. Which means they're expensive. Lose one in the grass or the pines and you're going to be spending the rest of the day looking for it."

"Is that a threat?"

"That's an added inducement to try to hit the target. Okay, remember that the trick is to combine a relaxation of the muscles in the hand drawing the bowstring at the same moment that you need maximum concentration on aiming. Just relax and release the arrow gently. Hold the release position until the arrow reaches the target."

"Or until it misses the target completely," Brenna sighed as the first one went wide.

"It takes practice. Don't worry about the arrow, I've got it spotted over there near that tree. Try another."

The thrill of having a few actually strike the target was greater than Brenna would have expected. She was elated and not a little exhausted a long time later as she walked with Ryder toward the target to remove the few that had managed to find their way in the right direction.

"Craig would love this," she remarked enthusiastically, inserting the arrows back into the quiver as he handed them to her.

"Craig?" There was a tight curiosity underlying the neutralness of the question. Brenna heard it and smiled to herself.

"My brother. He's going to be starting his senior year at the University of California at Berkeley this fall," she told him.

"You sound proud."

"I am. He's a good kid."

"If he's almost a senior in college, he should be a good *man* by now," Ryder observed, giving her a strange glance.

"He is." She smiled easily. "Sometimes I lapse, I'm afraid. There are a lot of years between us. He's only twenty and I'm twenty-nine. It's hard not to keep thinking of him as a kid brother."

"You sound as if you're pretty close to him."

"After Mom and Dad were killed a few years ago, all we had was each other," Brenna explained quietly as they walked back toward her cabin.

"With that much difference in your ages you must have wound up more or less raising him through his late teens," Ryder said thoughtfully.

"It was a struggle sometimes." She laughed, thinking about those years. "But Craig was a very responsible kid and he always seemed to keep in mind that I was a sibling, not a parent. He didn't deliberately challenge me the way real parents get challenged by teenagers, if you know what I mean."

"I know. Not from personal experience, because I've never had kids, but I've seen it in others," he admitted. "The Gardners, as a matter of fact, had a little trouble with their oldest boy a couple of years ago."

"But he got straightened out?" she asked with idle curiosity.

"Yes."

She looked up, intending to ask another question about the Gardners, but Ryder was already turning the conversation toward lunch.

And somehow lunch turned into an afternoon walk along the lakeshore in front of the cabins as she and Ryder explored a few of the picturesque coves and beaches that dotted the shoreline. The mellow warmth of the day hung on until the sun finally began to set behind the soaring peaks to the west. Then, regardless of her firm intention to the contrary, Brenna found herself sharing a whiskey sour with her neighbor as he broiled steaks over the barbecue on his back patio.

When she went back to her own cabin after dinner, there was an element of peace in the atmosphere between herself and Ryder. He dropped the smallest of brushing kisses against her mouth before seeing her safely inside, but it was a calm, good-night salute. It reminded her a little of the impersonal touch he had used when he'd searched her that first evening.

I was, she reflected uneasily, a little confusing. She had half expected to find herself fighting him off at the door. Given his aggressive nature and his apparent interest in pursuing a summer flirtation, it seemed logical.

So why did she feel a little let down? she demanded briskly of herself as she went about climbing the stairs to her loft bedroom. She should be grateful that he wasn't going to be the pushy type!

The next day she pulled out some of her notes and thought about outlining her fall classes. But that only brought back memories of the decision she had to make that summer. It was difficult, Brenna discovered, planning course work for her students when there was a possibility that she would not even be returning to the college!

Conscious of the stylish casualness of Lake Tahoe in the summer, she selected one of her few dresses with care that evening. After all, she told herself, she wanted the Gardners to have a good impression of their tenant! It was a perfect, summery white eyelet with full sleeves and a skirt that stopped at the knee. The dress was held low at the waist with a narrow sash of bright red, and she paired it with her red sandals, relying on the darkness of her sleekly knotted hair to provide the final touch of contrast.

It wasn't until Ryder knocked at her door that she admitted she might have dressed as much for him as for impressing the Gardners. She found the notion disturbing.

"Good evening," she began with the sort of cheery enthusiasm she imagined appropriate to a friendly date. As she caught sight of him after flinging open the door, her amber eyes widened first in surprise and then in appreciation of the picture he made on her doorstep.

"Don't tell me," she drawled, taking in his attire with a complete head-to-toe glance. "Your heroes not only get to drink the best brandy, they also buy their clothes from Italian designers!"

Not everyone could have worn the crisply tailored linen jacket in the palest of gray-blues, the narrow-legged white linen trousers, or the royal-blue silk shirt with such nonchalance. Ryder carried it off beautifully.

"You only live once," he responded easily. "And it does go with the Ferrari, don't you think?"

"Oh, yes, definitely," she agreed, laughing up at him as they started toward his car, which had been parked at the back of the cabin on the night she'd arrived. The Ferrari was a vivid red that, Brenna realized in amusement, was going to nicely complement her sash and sandals!

"You look very good tonight, lady," Ryder whispered as he assisted her into the cockpit of the beautifully designed automobile. She glanced up as she swung her bare legs inside, and the silver mesh of his eyes seemed to snag her gaze for a moment. She knew what the next question was going to be even before he asked it. "All for me?" He half smiled, taking in the whole of her with a leashed hunger.

"I wanted to impress my landlords," she retorted brightly, determined not to be drawn into such an admission. What was it with this man, anyway? She was beginning to realize she couldn't quite figure him out. A part of her warned that he was capable of reaching out and taking what he wanted, and that restrained hunger in him indicated that he wanted her. Yet other than that exploratory kiss yesterday morning and that quite mild good-night salute last night, there were few indications that she was going to have to fight him off.

The conflicting signals she was receiving both intrigued her and made her wary. She must remember that he wasn't from her world. He operated under a different set of rules than the average college professor or graduate student. It was best to keep a certain distance between them, and he seemed willing to cooperate.

But she wasn't fully aware of just how different Ryder Sterne's world was until she was introduced to Adam and Sue Gardner. A middle-aged couple of charm and affluence, they greeted Brenna with delight.

"Do come in, we're so pleased to meet you!" Sue Gardner exclaimed graciously as she welcomed her guests into the lovely lakeside home. "When Ryder phoned to say he was bringing you, we were so pleased! This is my husband, Adam.''

Adam proved to be a handsome man with a wealth of graying hair and a friendly, open smile. His wife was equally attractive. Both had that country-club look of health. Brenna couldn't help wondering how they had met Ryder. She couldn't really imagine him coming from their polished world of business success and prestige. No matter how well he wore his designer clothes, Brenna was certain he hadn't sprung from that kind of background.

Yet there was no doubting the pleasure the Gardners took in greeting her escort nor the obvious, almost maternal affection with which Sue Gardner kissed Ryder on the cheek.

''It's so good to see you, Ryder. I'm glad you were able to take advantage of the cabin again this year.'' She smiled, leading everyone onto the front deck, which soared outward toward the water.

''It makes a nice change from the apartment in Los Angeles, and you know damn well I can't beat the terms of your lease!'' Ryder accepted the salt-rimmed margarita Adam Gardner handed him. ''Actually I'm enjoying myself more this year than last. Your taste in tenants for the other cabin is improving,'' he said with a meaningful glance at Brenna, who occupied herself with demurely tasting the tart tequila drink she had just been handed.

Adam laughed. '' The luck of the draw, I'm afraid. Wish we could take credit, but it was all in the hands of the rental agent.''

''Brenna doesn't believe in fate so she probably doesn't believe in luck, either,'' Ryder murmured.

"Which leaves sheer chance," Brenna said firmly, deciding to take charge of the conversation before the two men ran it downhill at her expense. "Do you come up here every year, Ryder?"

There was a pause and the hesitation startled her. The Gardners seemed surprised at the question, and Ryder looked as if he wanted to head off the answer. But he was given no chance. Sue Gardner threw a very warm, very grateful smile at her guest and then turned to Brenna, who was beginning to feel as if she had accidentally tread on awkward ground.

"The cabin is available to Ryder anytime he wants it, Brenna," Sue said calmly. "We are only too glad when he takes advantage of it."

"I see." Brenna knew her tone sounded a little blank but there wasn't much she could do about it. She simply didn't understand the undercurrents that had begun to flow between the other three on the redwood deck.

"Hasn't Ryder explained about us?" Adam asked with a glance at the younger man. Then he answered his own question as Ryder's mouth hardened. "No, I can see he hasn't. We are very deeply in his debt, Brenna."

She frowned her lack of understanding, switching her questioning gaze to Ryder, who was ignoring all of them now. He sauntered to the railing and stood leaning on it, his eyes on a boat that was roaring across the lake trailing two water skiers. She had the distinct impression that he wanted to get the next few minutes over with in a hurry.

"He saved our son."

Brenna's gaze swung back to Adam's faintly smiling features. "Oh," she blurted out.

Surprisingly it was Ryder who spoke next, his voice distant and remote. "Brenna doesn't approve of this sort of thing. I think that's enough for now, Adam." He kept his gaze on the lake.

"But, Ryder, that's ridiculous! How could I not approve of your saving a boy's life?" She turned back to Adam Gardner. "What happened?"

Adam seemed torn between wanting to answer her and his obligation to respect Ryder's wishes. It was Sue who resolved the matter.

"He led a small group of hand-picked mercenaries in an assault on a prison in South America where Evan was being held on drug charges. The regime in power at the time was not at all sympathetic to U.S. citizens, and we were told we would probably never see our son again once he disappeared inside that prison," Sue Gardner explained quietly. "Ryder got him out and brought him home."

The margarita in Brenna's fingers sloshed precariously as she absorbed the full implications of the story. "Oh, my God!" Her attention went to the silent man at the rail. "You make a living doing things like that?" she breathed.

He swung around and caught her bemused expression. "I make a living writing books," he stated with a trace of challenge. He swirled the margarita in his glass and took a man-sized swallow.

"Books that relate your own exploits?" she persisted, shocked at what had been revealed about him. Somehow she had thought the violent side of him was safely confined to his adventure fiction. Now she knew it existed in real life, too.

"Brenna, he was doing us an incredible favor," Adam Gardner put in deliberately, sensing the tension in her reaction. "He's not exactly a paid mercenary."

And suddenly Ryder was grinning, that wide, slashing, wicked grin that had such a strange effect on Brenna. This time there was a fierce challenge in it as his eyes met hers. "Not exactly," he agreed very distinctly, swallowing the remainder of his margarita. "Not anymore. Now I am a writer of sleazy men's fiction. Period. Let's eat."

Three

"I'll have to admit you recovered very nicely and maintained your end of the social repartee for the remainder of the evening," Ryder told Brenna much later that night as he helped her back into the front seat of the red Ferrari. "But I imagine you're just about to burst, so why don't you go ahead and get it over with?"

Brenna slanted him an assessing glance as he slid into the seat beside her. She was aware of the challenge in him. It had been radiating from him ever since the full truth about his rather violent past had come out. He was virtually daring her to hold it against him. For some reason, perhaps because of several margaritas and a swing in her mood toward objectivity, she found that amusing and a little touching.

"You think I'm going to chew you out because you saved some kid's neck?"

There was a small hesitation. ''He wasn't guilty, you know,'' Ryder finally said in an even, almost conversational tone. He watched the winding road with care, seemingly totally occupied with his steering. ''He got involved with some people who used him. Set out to see the world and escape from his parents' lifestyle and got more than hc bargained for. You'd like him now. He's a stockbroker!''

Brenna smiled. ''Thank God Craig never decided to defy all authority and see the world!''

''You must have handled him well.''

''The only things that's worrying me is that he's not particularly happy at the university.'' Brenna sighed. ''But I think I've convinced him to finish now that he's come this far.''

She sensed Ryder taking a long breath as if to steady himself. ''Can I take it that I'm not in for a long lecture on the evils of my rough-and-ready past?''

''It's not my place to lecture you, Ryder.''

''Please don't be condescending,'' he warned very quietly.

Brenna thought about that. Was she being condescending? ''How did the Gardners find you when they, uh, needed someone to get their son out of that prison?'' she surprised herself by asking.

''I was an officer in the Marines. Served in Southeast Asia and later in…other places. When I left the service to start writing full time, it occasionally became convenient to pick up a little extra money. I kept in touch with some friends I'd made in the service. There's a kind of network out there, Brenna, and when people like the Gardners start looking for help, it can be found. Getting in and out of awkward places is something I happen to be good at,'' he added with a disparaging shrug.

''And perhaps something you like doing?'' Brenna smiled perceptively.

''Not anymore. I'm satisfied with the writing these days,'' he told her in a tone that once again dared her to contradict.

Brenna's smile widened as she drank in the crisp mountain air through her open window. She felt good tonight. It was good to be driving around the lake with a man who was totally different from any she had known. It was as if she were someone else this evening, and she wanted the illusion to continue for a time.

''Does that mean I am out tonight with a successful author of sleazy men's fiction rather than an ex-soldier-of-fortune?'' she teased lightly.

He flicker her a quick, almost uncertain glance. ''Yes.''

''Good. Talk to me of storytelling, Ryder Sterne. Or is it Justin Murdock?'' she corrected, thinking of his pseudonym.

''Would you mind a personal question?''

''Not at all, not at all,'' she assured him happily.

''How many of those margaritas did you have tonight?''

''I'm not drunk,'' she declared, aware that she sounded vaguely defensive about it. But she wasn't, not really. She was just feeling temporarily free and vitally aware of the man beside her. She'd never been aware of Damon in quite this way. Why was that? she wondered silently.

"Then why don't we try our hand at cards tonight, lady?" Ryder suggested. "I'll stop at one of the casinos and we can see if your philosophy does you any good when it goes against luck, one on one."

"That sounds...different. Yes, I think I'd like that."

Brenna didn't hear the dreaminess in her voice but she felt it in her mind. A wonderful sense of being in another reality. As if she had somehow stepped into a different plane of existence just for this evening.

As for Ryder, she had the impression that some burden had been lifted from him. He sounded happier suddenly; more than willing to forget the discussion of his past and devote himself to the remainder of the evening.

"I feel lucky tonight," he told her as he parked the Ferrari in one of the lots of a luxurious, highrise casino-hotel in the south-shore town of Stateline. "Luckier than I have for a long time." He helped her gallantly out of the car and took her arm as they walked toward the brilliantly lit casino. "What do you call luck in your world, lady?"

Brenna's lips curved invitingly. "Well, there is something known as the probability theory. Otherwise called chance."

"Close enough," he proclaimed as they stepped through the casino doors.

Before them lay the glitter, the excitement, and the pleasure-bent crowds of a big Nevada casino. The chandeliers, well-dressed croupiers, and scantily clad cocktail waitresses all combined with the tinkling of slot machines and the spin of a wheel of fortune to add to Brenna's glow of unreality. There was an overstated aura of luxury that seemed to swallow one up and form a world of its own. It suited Brenna's unusual mood exactly.

She clung gracefully to Ryder's arm as he led her onto the gambling floor. Even if she had not felt like clinging that night, Brenna wasn't certain she would have been able to free herself. Ryder was ensuring her proximity with a possessive grip that was inordinately pleasing to her senses. Damon never kept her close like this when they went out together. Dr. Fielding didn't believe in archaic masculine emotions such as possessiveness. Normally, Brenna tried to remind herself, she didn't believe in such notions, either. But tonight was different. Perhaps because the man involved was different.

"Do you know how to play any of the card games?" Ryder asked, glancing down at her animated expression with a warm, amused look in his eyes.

"No, I'll watch you for a while. I think the slot machines are going to be more my speed."

"Stand close behind me and we'll see just how much good luck you're capable of bringing me tonight," he drawled, taking a place at one of the green baize-topped tables. The young and attractive woman dealing the cards turned a very brilliant smile on her latest customer.

"I think the croupier is trying to make a pass at you," Brenna warned Ryder in a dramatically low tone.

"Nonsense." Ryder grinned cheerfully. "She's paid to smile like that at everyone. Now keep very quiet while we're playing and put your hand on my shoulder so I'll know you're there.''

"You think the hand on the shoulder is necessary?''

"It's how the luck gets channeled from you to me,'' he explained.

"Oh.''

And then it was too late to say anything else. The attractive croupier began to deal the cards and Ryder gave the game his full attention. Brenna dutifully kept her crimson nails resting lightly on the pale blue-gray jacket shoulder and watched in fascination. Ryder played with the professionalism with which he did everything else, she thought fleetingly. Fully alert but serenely in control of himself and, apparently, of his luck. He was winning.

"There you go,'' he concluded, pocketing his chips at last and turning away from the table. ''What did I tell you? Tonight is my lucky night. Come on, lady, let's go find another game to play.''

At the wheel of fortune Brenna took a chance herself, putting an entire dollar onto the number she had chosen. When it came back doubled, she lifted happy, glowing eyes to Ryder, who was standing close, his arm around her waist.

"This could be an easier way to make a living than teaching philosophy,'' she announced.

He laughed. "Is teaching philosophy so hard?''

That question brought back unwelcome reminders of the real world waiting for her at the start of the fall semester. "It isn't the teaching that's so bad, it's…never mind. I want to try the slots!''

He made no attempt to force her back into the

unpleasant path the conversation was taking, guiding her instead to the nearest of a bank of quarter slots. There she began to plunk in quarters with an enthusiasm that would have astounded her at another time.

"Somehow it doesn't seem like real money here," she explained apologetically as the machine politely gobbled up quarter after quarter. The apology in her voice was due to the fact that it was Ryder who had financed her go at the slots.

"Go on trying," he instructed, unperturbed. "I keep telling you we can't lose tonight."

With the next quarter he was proved correct. Instead of swallowing it and waiting implacably for the next feeding, the machine began to tinkle with the delightful sound of cascading quarters.

"Ryder, look! We're rich!"

"I'll get a cup to put the loot in," he said, grinning.

Brenna stood trying to estimate her winnings as he disappeared momentarily and then returned with a cardboard cup. Laughing with delight, Brenna scooped the coins into it.

"We'll never be able to carry all this!"

"All we have to do is get it as far as the cashier's stand. They'll turn it into nice lightweight bills," he told her.

"The casino management will probably ask us politely to leave if we keep this up." Brenna chuckled as they moved off down the aisle of slot machines.

"A couple of hundred bucks isn't going to break them. Still, maybe we should take a little time out."

"I thought you were supposed to stick with a hot streak once you had one going," she protested.

"Oh, I intend to pursue the hot streak. On the dance floor."

Brenna thought about that as he guided her toward the lounge that overlooked the gambling floor. A sophisticated trio was playing while more of the scantily clad waitresses moved back and forth among the intimate cocktail tables. She thought about it carefully, trying to analyze the situation. For the first time that evening she asked herself silently what she might be getting into, but when Ryder took her in his arms, the questions faded back beyond the edges of the pleasant dream world she was inhabiting this evening.

He wrapped her close, the possessiveness she had sensed in him all evening seeming to escalate by several quantum leaps. His hand moved down her back to the base of her spine, pressing her audaciously into his warmth. Ryder's breath moved a tiny, loose tendril of hair as he inhaled the scent of her. Without protest, Brenna settled her head on his strong shoulder.

"Enjoying yourself this evening, lady?" he growled very softly.

"Yes," she admitted unhesitatingly. "Very much. And you?"

"I thought things were going to be a bit rough for a while but now everything seems to be going smoothly, doesn't it? Yes, I'm enjoying myself. I'm enjoying *you*. I think I mentioned once before that I like the feel of you under my hands."

An unexpected tremor went through her as he suited action to words and moved his fingers compellingly along her spine. Brenna found herself drinking in the feel of his hard body, the totally male fragrance of his skin, and the indefinable, incredibly complex combination of factors that were attracting her senses. It was a magic night, made even more so because she didn't believe in magic. With a sense of curiosity and desire she moved her nails lightly at the back of his neck, twisting her fingers delicately in the tawny depths of his hair.

His reaction was immediate and electric. His hold on her tightened and his deep voice became very soft indeed. The whisper of silk on a knife blade, Brenna thought, intrigued. What was it about Ryder's voice that she should remember?

"Dangerous," she suddenly said dreamily, her eyes closing.

"What's dangerous?"

"You are when your voice gets very gentle and soft." She smiled without lifting her lashes.

"I'm not the one who's dangerous tonight," he whispered, finding the curve of her ear with the tip of his tongue in a quick, sensuous tasting action. "You're the one who represents a real threat."

"Hah!" She snuggled closer, moving her fingers on the back of his neck this time just inside the line of his collar. "I am a prudent, circumspect, well-behaved faculty member of a very respected college."

"Who goes around climbing through the bedroom windows of unsuspecting males and seducing them on the dance floor," Ryder concluded for her throatily.

"I am not," Brenna stated categorically, "seducing you!"

"That's a matter of opinion."

Brenna opened her eyes and found him watching her face with an intensity that stirred her senses. "Do you feel seduced?" she asked interestedly.

"I feel as though I were being swept out into the middle of Lake Tahoe. It's very deep out in the middle of the lake, lady. A man could be dragged under and never find his way back to the surface," Ryder murmured, his voice vibrating with the purr of a lion.

"I have the feeling you're a very strong swimmer."

"The danger is that I might not want to swim away in time."

"Is this some sort of cryptic warning?" Brenna dared.

"Perhaps."

"A cryptic warning," she repeated wisely. "Then I shall have to be very careful, won't I?"

His shoulder lifted easily in a movement that suggested the matter was out of his hands. "Perhaps. Then again, if it's all a twist of fate, nothing you do will have much effect."

"You forget that I don't believe in fate."

"In which case you're stuck having to take full responsibility for your own actions, aren't you?" he taunted huskily, inclining his head to drop the smallest of suggestive little kisses on the curve of her throat.

"I," she announced bravely, aware of a pleasant warmth creeping through her veins, "am a great believer in personal responsibility."

"So am I," he returned. "Because even when fate and luck are involved, there are always choices to be made. The choice tonight will be yours, lady. Think twice before you select the riskier option, because I will hold you to it."

"Another cryptic warning?" she teased.

"I suppose," he sighed and pulled her closer.

They danced several more numbers and Brenna found herself surrendering to the natural grace of his body. She had the feeling that she wasn't nearly as coordinated, even though no one had ever thought her ungraceful. But he made it easy to slide into the pattern of his rhythm, and once into it, she didn't want to back out.

"It's nearly two," Ryder said at last as they walked off the floor and back to their small table.

"Really?" Brenna stifled a delicate little yawn. "Time for me to be crawling through somebody's window, hmmm?"

"Not unless it's mine. Are you ready to go home?"

"Yes." She took another look at the still-lively casino gambling floor. "Don't these places ever close?"

"No. Come, lady. Let's go home to bed."

She looked up at that as he got to his feet beside her, searching his voice and expression for innuendos and double meanings. But Ryder merely smiled back, taking her arm and leading her through the casino and out into the parking lot.

Safely inside the cockpit of the red Ferrari, Brenna leaned her head back against the leather seat and watched the passing scenery of night-darkened pines and lake with a pleasant, floating feeling. Ryder didn't speak as he drove, but she was aware of a sense of closeness that didn't seem to need words. A man apart. Different, complex, intriguing. But there was a vulnerability in him, she thought fleetingly. A vulnerability he tried to mask with self-confidence and self-reliance. She had seen it briefly this evening after the truth about his past had emerged.

"Did you want me to know, Ryder?" she whispered suddenly.

"Know what?"

"About the way you used to make your living."

He hesitated. "I'm not sure. I told myself it would be better if you didn't find out, but then I found myself taking you to meet the Gardners. A part of me must have guessed the truth would come out there. I guess I must have wanted it out in the open before things went very far between us."

"A question of honor?" she chided gently.

"In a way," he replied evenly.

"Admirable." She nodded, smiling. "But you needn't have worried."

"Because you're not going to hold it against me?" He slid her an enigmatic glance.

"No, because things aren't going to go so far between us that it will matter," she retorted lightly, knowing that her response was a kind of challenge.

But it was a challenge he evidently didn't intend to pick up. Ryder said nothing, concentrating on his driving.

He still said nothing as he parked the Ferrari and walked her to her front porch. Then he turned to her and spoke with gentle urgency.

"Invite me in, lady. For a nightcap."

She met his eyes, aware of her own quickening

pulse and the sensuous silver of his gaze. ''I...I don't have any brandy.''

''Tea will be fine.''

For a moment the force of his will seemed to collide with the wavering shield of her ambivalence. It was a contest in which ambivalence stood little or no chance. Fingers trembling ever so slightly with an excitement and a fear she didn't want to name, Brenna handed him her key.

Without a word he inserted it in the lock and pushed open the door.

''I'll build a fire,'' he said as he closed the door with a decisiveness that made the creeping warmth in Brenna's veins flare a little hotter. She watched him move across the room with that easy, catlike stride and then she turned and went toward the kitchen.

A few minutes later she stood staring unseeingly at the teakettle, waiting for the water to boil and listening to the sounds of Ryder constructing the fire. What was she doing? Did she even want to think about it?

An air of inevitability settled on her. It was something that seemed to have been enveloping her for most of the evening but that she had deliberately avoided facing. It was easier to take each event as it occurred even though common sense saw the ultimate conclusion to the pattern that was forming. Brenna poured the tea water over the leaves in the ceramic pot and prepared a tray with cups and saucers.

She found Ryder sprawled on the sofa, staring into the fire as she emerged from the kitchen with her tray. He looked up as she came forward, silvery eyes roving over her with a muted hunger that couldn't quite be hidden. It was a hunger that found an answering response deep in Brenna, and the cups rattled a little as she set down the tray on the round wicker table.

"To a night of decadent pleasure," she toasted with a determined lightness as she poured the tea and handed him his cup.

"Philosophy professors don't usually spend their summer evenings cavorting in gambling dens with writers of sleazy men's fiction?" Ryder queried dryly as he took the cup.

"I don't. Not usually," she stated calmly, lashes dropping as she sipped the soothing brew.

"Come now, surely there have been philosophers who have argued in favor of what is commonly referred to as the good life?" Ryder seemed willing to follow her mood. That surprised Brenna a little. But it fit in with the conflicting signals she had received before from him. She could be absolutely certain one moment that he wanted her and in the next he made it clear that she could set the pace and determine the direction. She didn't quite understand.

"Oh, there have been several who advocated a life of pleasure, but I'm afraid they had the pleasures of intellectual discovery in mind, not the more worldly ones," she lectured flippantly. "Even poor, maligned Epicurus was much more concerned with the pleasure of the pursuit of knowledge than the pleasures of the body. His opponents were the ones who made the world 'epicurean' a byword for a luxurious lifestyle. Epicurus and his circle of followers were really quite restrained. Even so, I suppose he was a little radical compared to some of the others who advocated a very stoic existence,'' she finished speculatively, glancing into the fire.

"Nevertheless," Ryder persisted softly, "there are philosophical theories that could be used to justify either life in the fast lane or a more cerebral existence?''

"Probably," Brenna agreed with a small smile.

"And a man trying to decide which path to follow is allowed the choice?''

"There's always the doctrine of free will," she acknowledged, amused.

He set down his teacup and removed the one in her hands. "Then I choose to kiss you and the hell with the risks.''

Brenna held her breath, her nerves tingling and alive as he swept her into his arms. She made no protest when his mouth came searchingly down on hers. She wasn't certain in that moment that she *could* have made a protest. This was where the evening had been leading, and she knew she wanted to taste a little of what this man had to offer her senses. The urge to do so was overpowering.

The first thing she realized as he wrapped her against him was that the hunger in him was still leashed. She felt that hunger in the hardness of his body, knew it in the warmth of his mouth, but it was under control. A deep feminine instinct made her want to be the woman who could release and satisfy that hunger.

The knowledge shook her and the trembling in her

slender frame seemed to seek solace from the rising heat of his passion.

When his lips moved persuasively on hers, Brenna lifted her arms to encircle his neck as she opened her mouth to him. His questing tongue surged inside with a reckless aggression that thrilled her. He explored the warm, wet secrets behind her lips with an arousing, exciting boldness that left her the hungry one.

She sank heavily against him and he accepted the weight of her, letting it carry them both backward until she was lying on top of him. When Brenna tried to catch her breath and her common sense, he tangled her legs in his own and held her head close.

''A little more,'' he breathed huskily and she obeyed. Of their own volition her tender hands framed the rough, craggy planes of his face as she responded to the kiss. Her mind was whirling with the sensual pleasures that beckoned and seduced. He was altogether different, and she felt compelled to explore whatever it was he offered.

Their tongues met in an intricate dance of primitive courtship as Ryder flattened his palms along her back and began to stroke her in long, rhythmic motions. Unconsciously Brenna's body arched into him in response, glorying in the lean strength awaiting her.

When she moaned, he drank the sound from her throat as if it were nectar and then he asked for more. Her small, muffled cry came once more, and this time he splayed his fingers across the curve of her hips and forced her gently against his thighs.

With that sensual contact Brenna was made fiercely aware of the thrusting, potent strength of his desire. The dazzling surge of excitement through her body suffused it with a warm flush that seemed to elevate her temperature. He wanted her and heaven help her, she wanted him! Never had it been like this. Never had a man fascinated and intrigued her in quite this way. She wanted to forget about the future and the past and do anything in her power to continue in this delightful plane of unreality.

"Ryder?" His name was a question and a plea on her lips as she lifted her head an inch to meet his eyes.

The tawny lashes rose, revealing the molten silver behind them. He looked deeply into her drugged and dream-filled gaze for a long moment.

"I told you on the dance floor that the choice would be yours tonight, lady," he said with dark velvet in his words. "Just remember that I will hold you to your decision if you choose to take the risk."

"What risk?"

"The risk of inviting me into your bed."

Hearing it spelled out so bluntly sent a tremor through her but she managed not to lower her lashes in spite of the confusion she was experiencing. "What is the risk, Ryder? That you won't stay long in my bed?" she provoked deliberately, ignoring the pain of that possibility.

His mouth crooked and he lifted his fingers to spear them through the sleek knot of her hair, dislodging the clip. "No, you little idiot, the risk you're taking is that I will stay there. Don't you understand, Brenna? I won't let you go after I've made you mine. Hell, I might not let you go even if you back away entirely tonight!" he ended forcefully.

''What are you talking about?'' she whispered.

''I'm talking about commitment, and the fact that you have to ask the question means it's probably much too soon for me to claim you. It means you're probably not thinking in those terms.'' He twisted his hands through her unloosened hair and his mouth continued to smile gently even though his eyes were gleaming and largely unreadable.

''You want a…a commitment from me? That's something of a switch, isn't it?'' she tried to ask mockingly and failed miserably. Her amber gaze was darkening with tension and the unknown aspects of the moment. ''Isn't it usually the woman who—'' She broke off, unable to continue. Her crimson nails dug anxiously into the blue silk shirt.

''I'm not concerned with how it 'usually' is,'' he rasped. ''I'm only concerned with how it is for me and you. I want you, Brenna, but I'm willing to take the time to make it right for both of us. I'm willing to wait for you. I'm warning you that if you give yourself to me tonight, you won't find yourself free of me in the morning. Do you understand now? I won't play the part of a summer novelty for you to explore while you're running around outside your ivory tower.''

''No! I never meant…''

He shook his head. ''I know I represent a different world to you, and perhaps under the spell of the evening and your own curiosity you find yourself attracted. If that's all it amounts to, you'd better back away from the flames before you get singed.''

''It's not like that at all!'' she proclaimed fiercely, the need to reassure him somehow more important than a close look at the truth. "Believe me, Ryder, it's not like that..."

Knowing no other way to counter his accusation, Brenna caught his face once more in her hands and ground her mouth almost savagely down on his. She would not, could not, examine her options in the intellectual way she ought to. Brenna only knew that the night must not end with Ryder Sterne walking out her door.

Ryder's arms tightened around her with rough gentleness as he slowly sat up against the pressure of her slender weight. He never broke the kiss but Brenna found herself cradled across his thighs, her arms wound passionately around his neck.

Then, in a surge of masculine power, Ryder was on his feet with Brenna in his arms. Still holding her mouth in the compelling mastery of his own, he started toward the stairs of the loft.

Four

One of Brenna's high-heeled red sandals slipped off and fell on a step as Ryder carried her effortlessly up the stairs. She wasn't really aware of the small loss, but the toes of her nylon-clad foot curled in a tiny gesture of gathering sensual tension. Ryder's arms felt strong and secure about her, and she nestled against his chest in languid, delicious abandon.

At the top of the stairs he at last broke the enthralling, lingering kiss to lift his head and search her bemused, heavy-lidded expression.

"Tonight you're a golden-eyed witch," he told her huskily.

"And you?" she countered, touching the corner of his mouth with a fingertip. "What are you tonight?"

"Only a man. But one who wants you very much. Will that be enough for you?"

What was he asking? Brenna wondered distantly. Whatever the real question, she wanted nothing more than to reassure him.

"It will be enough." Perhaps he was concerned that she would ask too much of him, demand more than he could give. Yet he had been the one who had talked of commitment. She didn't understand but she didn't want to get too involved in an analysis of the situation, either. Not now, not tonight. Tonight was a special place and a special time and she wanted only to exist within those borders. "Ryder, I'm not truly a witch. Only a woman. Will that be enough for you?" she heard herself ask a little anxiously.

"It's all I want," he whispered, his voice as deep and gentle as she had yet heard it.

He carried her to the bed and lowered her carefully to her feet beside it.

"Oh!" The small exclamation came as Brenna stumbled slightly against him and instinctively braced herself with palms splayed across his shoulders.

"What's wrong?" He steadied her at once.

"My shoe." She smiled in soft amusement. "I seem to have arrived with only one."

"Playing at being Cinderella after the ball?" He eased her to a sitting position on the edge of the bed and went down on one knee in front of her.

"Only if you're interested in the Prince Charming role," she tried to say nonchalantly and was very much afraid she failed.

She didn't feel nonchalant tonight. She felt elated, nervous, passionate, and high-strung. She felt a dizzying conglomeration of emotions but she didn't feel at all nonchalant.

"No, I'm not quite right for that role." Deliberately Ryder put his hand on her uncovered knee and slid it silkily down her calf to the foot that still wore a shoe. Slowly he began to unfasten the buckle of the tiny red strap. "I'm much more interested in undressing you than I am in finding you a slipper that fits. Tonight I'd make a lousy Prince Charming." His mouth twisted in a wry self-mockery that touched her heart.

Instinctively Brenna threaded her hands through his hair and moved them slowly down to rest on his shoulders. An unbidden, feminine perception told her that he was asking obliquely for reassurance of her desire for him. How could she refuse? Tonight she wanted to give this man everything he asked.

He looked up at her from under the tawny lashes and she smiled tenderly. "Tonight you're a perfect Prince Charming. Exactly as I always thought Prince Charming would be."

Without a word he lifted his hands to pull her head down to his, and this time she knew from his kiss that the hunger she sensed in him was rapidly coming unbound. Why had he maintained it under such restraint? A man's desire, she had always thought, was a relatively simple thing and certainly not something he bothered to conceal or control when the opportunity to indulge it occurred.

But Ryder was different and the quality of his desire was different. She felt a hunger that was not strictly sexual underlying it and knew a fierce joy at being the one who could unleash it.

When she moaned throatily under the impact of the spiraling kiss, Ryder lowered one hand to trace the distance from her shoulder to the tip of her breast. He drew in his breath sharply when he discovered the taut outline of her nipple and pushed her back against the quilt.. He followed, coming down heavily beside her while he continued to move his thumb provocatively against the sensitive peak.

Brenna arched upward, seeking more of his touch, and whispered his name softly into his mouth. His hand went to the bright red sash that held the white dress low on her hip. It loosened magically beneath his touch. Slowly he continued to undress her, finding the fastenings of the eyelet dress while he buried his mouth at the pulsepoint of her throat.

"Oh, Ryder!"

Brenna's head tipped back over his arm in silent supplication and surrender and her eyes shut tightly against the wonder of the moment. Everything was so perfect; he was so perfect.

"You're so exactly right for me," he grated in a velvet-gentle voice as the white dress slipped down to her waist and the curves of her breasts were revealed. Only the filmiest of lace and satin remained and the thrusting tips of her nipples were clearly outlined. "Small and sleek and sensuous."

He found the center clasp of the demicup bra and undid it. When the lacy covering fell aside, he groaned as he began to trail a string of kisses from the base of her throat to the rose-tipped crests.

"My little lady cat burglar," he whispered thickly as he stroked the length of her to her hips. "I wanted to do this the night you crawled through my window!''

''No,'' she protested even though the excitement was flaming through her at his words. ''You didn't want me like this. Not then…''

''You still don't know me that well, do you?''

But he gave her no chance to reply as he curled his tongue coaxingly around her nipple and traced a circle that made her breath catch in her throat. Her red-gilt nails sank into the shoulders beneath the blue silk shirt as she cried out.

Her response seemed to arouse him still further. In an swift, smooth movement he slid his palms down the curve of her hips, pushing the remainder of her clothing all the way to her ankles and off the bed. In one long, sweeping stroke she was suddenly and completely nude.

Brenna's eyes opened to find him drinking in the sight of her as his fingers went to the buttons of the blue shirt.

''No, let me,'' she managed, struggling to a sitting position and finding the buttons with fingers that trembled from passionate excitement.

The tawny lashes feathered his cheeks as he let his own hands fall aside. Ryder sat very still as she worked at the fastenings of the blue shirt. But when she slipped her palms beneath the open edges to find the curling hair that covered his bronzed chest, he muttered her name a little violently and caught her wrists.

''Brenna, my golden-eyed witch, you'll drive me crazy if I give you free rein! I want this to last all night!''

"I'm the one who will go crazy if you try to make it last forever," she protested huskily. "I...I *need* you too badly."

She bit off the words, a part of her astounded by them. She had never truly *needed* a man in quite this way. This was different than mere affection tinged with sexual attraction. This was different than the time in graduate school when she had thought she was truly in love. This was different than the way she felt toward Damon. She needed Ryder Sterne and she ached to please him.

"Do you, Brenna?" he growled in his dragon's purr. "Do you really need me?"

"More than anything else in the world," she answered with an honesty that would have surprised her in another context. She lifted her lashes and the gold in her eyes met the silver in his. He groaned in satisfaction and a kind of relief. She knew in that moment that the strange hunger in him was finally and completely unleashed. He made no further protest as she fumbled with the remainder of his clothes.

"You're beautiful," she breathed in wonder as he finally lay naked beside her. With delicate, questing fingertips she traced the shape of him, moving across the contours of his smoothly muscled chest, down to the flat stomach and over the muscular shape of his hip.

Unable to resist, she bent to kiss the center of his chest as her hand clenched a little aggressively into the hard male buttock. Instantly his fingers wrapped themselves in her hair and he pulled her forcibly up to find his mouth.

"We'll make the next time last," he promised

thickly against her mouth. "This time I'm not going to be able to play the gentleman!"

"Ryder!" His name was choked from her as, his hands still entwined in the depths of her bittersweet-chocolate hair, he moved, shifting her firmly onto her back. He sprawled heavily across her, his thigh pinning hers as he quenched his thirst at her mouth.

"I'm sorry, sweet lady," he muttered against her lips as he held her face cupped fiercely in his excitingly rough palms. "I meant to play the gallant lover but I can't. Not this first time with you. All I can think of now is making you mine completely and absolutely. Do you understand? I can't be sexually sophisticated tonight and impress you with my charm and gallantry. I want you too badly!"

Brenna couldn't answer. Her own passion was running too high and her senses seemed to swim. Her nails dug compellingly into his shoulders and she arched her hips against the pressure of his body. It was the only response she could manage.

It was enough. With a violently tender exclamation Ryder slid his palm over her breasts, down the small contour of her stomach, and found the tangled thicket below. He forced her legs gently apart with his knee and let his probing fingers discover the intimate secret of her.

When she writhed beneath him at the touch, he whispered her name hoarsely and pressed the hard strength of his body testingly against her thighs.

"Please. Ryder, please!"

"My God, sweet lady!"

He lifted himself, his shoulders looming briefly over her in the shadowy light, and then he settled himself along the length of her, fitting himself between her legs with a gentle aggression that sent shivers through Brenna's nerve endings.

She reached up, clinging to him as if he were all that mattered in the world, welcoming him completely.

He came to her with a bold power that shocked her senses. Her nails raked the contour of his back and his name was a silent cry of desire and passion on her lips as he held her with a strength she couldn't have defied even if she had been so inclined. Then he was surging against her body, taking it by storm and sweeping her along into a vortex of swirling color and sensation. Ryder Sterne made love as if he were staking a claim; tuning a fine instrument only to his personal touch; taming a wild creature. The experience overwhelmed and consumed Brenna's senses.

He established a rhythm to which she responded at once. She locked her arms and legs around his driving body, thrilling to the potent, sinewy feel of him. When her nails dug deeper in a convulsive reaction, he nipped passionately at the smooth flesh of her shoulder. The small, tingling pain only served to heighten her awareness to new levels.

Together they spun through their own private universe, so tightly entwined they were as one as they made the sensual journey. When the coiling, flickering tension in Brenna's loins began to flare out of control, she gulped for air and tensed in Ryder's hold.

"Ryder! Ryder, darling!"

He must have heard the amazement and wonder

and perhaps even an element of fear in her words as she faced the blazing conclusion of the trip.

"Let yourself go, lady," he rasped. "Give yourself to me!"

As if his words were the last impulse her body needed to send her over the edge, Brenna went abruptly taut beneath him, and then the explosion took her in a series of tiny convulsions that swept her from head to toe.

"Oh, Ryder!"

As if he, in turn, only needed her finish to spark his own, Ryder swept into her body once more, filling her completely and holding her with total possession as he reached the end of his journey.

Long moments later Brenna stirred beneath the heavy male body still covering her own. At the hint of movement Ryder lazily lifted his tousled, tawny head from her breast and looked down at her, the faintest of smiles edging his mouth. The molten silver in his eyes had cooled to be replaced by a warm satisfaction that pleased Brenna. She had fed the hunger in him.

They stared wonderingly at each other in silence for a time, each absorbing the fullness of the moment, and then Ryder ducked his head briefly to drop a tiny kiss on her love-softened mouth.

"I know this is going to sound ridiculous in the light of events, but when I picked you up at your door this evening, I honestly had no intention of winding up in your bed later," he confessed.

"Was it fate or free will?" she teased dreamily, playing with the perspiration-damp hair at the back of his neck.

"I don't know and I don't particularly care. It happened. That's all that matters now."

She opened her eyes a little wider at the forcefulness of the statement. "Are you upset about what happened, Ryder?" Please, no, she thought. She only wanted him to be happy!

"Of course not," he drawled, his expression softening at once. "It was a little too soon and involved some risks because of that, but perhaps there wasn't any other way it could have gone. You're mine now, Brenna. I've waited a long time to find you, lady, and now that I have I won't be letting you go."

"I'm not going anywhere. Not tonight," she soothed, uncertain of his meaning and unwilling to press for clarification. The night was too precious.

He stroked back the dark hair from her damp forehead and smiled with incredible gentleness. "No, you won't be going anywhere tonight." Then he shook his head once in amused bafflement. " A professor of philosophy. How could I have possibly guessed?"

"Guessed what?" she prompted curiously, enjoying the soothing touch of his fingers across her brow. She wriggled beneath him contentedly.

"That I'd find the woman I wanted and needed, the one who understood about things like honor and the one who was capable of sending me out of my head with desire, on the faculty of some small college of which I had never heard. Hell, Brenna," he added with a wry chuckle deep in his throat. "I finished college in the Marine Corps, and I can assure you there wasn't much attention paid to subjects like ethics and philosophy!"

"A limited education?"

"A practical education," he corrected with a small grin. He lowered his head for another nibbling kiss, drawing back with some reluctance. "Are you happy with the results of your seductive techniques tonight, lady?" he taunted lightly.

"I refuse to answer on the grounds that it might tend to incriminate me," she murmured, drawing inviting little circles on his upper arms.

"Well," he retorted deliberately, "I suppose it doesn't much matter whether or not I manage to drag a confession out of you. It's done. You're mine."

Brenna thought about that, aware of the determination in him and not quite comprehending his full meaning. He was a possessive man, it would seem. And tonight he possessed her. She didn't want to think any further than that.

"Don't go to sleep on me, witch," he drawled humorously as her lashed lowered to her cheeks. "That first time was to settle the issue. Now that it's settled, I'm going to take the time to make a good impression."

Her mouth curved. "Is that a threat?"

"Just try to stay awake so you can applaud the performance, okay?"

He shaped her head with his fingers and lowered his mouth once more to hers. This time his kiss was slow and lingeringly passionate as he set about stoking the banked fires back to shimmering brightness.

Ryder took his time, as promised, moving over her languid body with finesse and an arousing strength that pushed aside the remnants of earlier passion and set about creating a new experience. She was stroked from breast to thigh, teased with sensitive fingers that knew exactly where to tempt and tantalize. And his kisses, she thought deliriously, his kisses were a sweet ravishment. He poured them without restraint across the roundness of her breasts, dropped them delicately onto the softness of her stomach, and branded them into the exquisitely tender skin of her inner thighs. Brenna had temporarily lost herself in his arms the last time. This time she thought she might never find her way back out.

When he came to her at last, enveloping her in his warmth, she never gave another thought to the prospect of being permanently lost. He flowed into her body and across it and there was no way she could have resisted. This time, when the shimmering conclusion approached, she gave herself up to it without any fear at all, welcoming the flames of surrender in the safety of Ryder's arms.

When it was over he turned her gently on her side, pulled her tightly into the curve of his glisteningly damp body, and ordered her to sleep in the softest of whispers.

"Ryder, I feel like I'm floating."

"So do I. Go to sleep, lady."

"Why?"

"Because that's what I'm going to do and I can't bear the thought of you lying awake staring at the ceiling while I'm snoring blissfully!"

"Oh, dear. Do you snore?" She chuckled.

"It's a little late to worry about it. Tonight you've agreed to take the good with the bad." He yawned, nestling his head against hers.

"Tonight's almost over, Ryder," she pointed out wistfully.

"There's tomorrow to look forward to. Good night, sweet lady."

"Good night, Prince Charming."

He laughed sleepily and then he was asleep. A moment later so was Brenna.

She awoke the next morning in a warm, tousled bed, the down quilt snuggled close to her chin. Her first impression was that something was wrong.

Brenna's eyes opened slowly to find the sunlight filtering brightly through the window cut in the peaked roof. It was late. But that wasn't what was wrong. Her legs stretched idly and she became aware of a faint soreness in the muscles of her thighs.

Not an unpleasant sensation in and of itself, but it brought back memories of the night with alarming speed. Brenna struggled to a sitting position, glancing around her bedroom with a kind of fear. Where was Ryder?

It wasn't his absence that seemed wrong, it was the possibility that he would step out of the bathroom or come up the stairs with breakfast at any minute that sent a wave of panic through her senses.

My God! What had she done last night? She must have been out of her mind! With heartfelt anxiety she tossed back the quilt and stumbled to her feet, chilled in the morning light. Shakily she reached for the fluffy, high-necked, saffron-colored robe lying across the foot of the bed. It was only as she belted it on that she remembered it hadn't been there last night. Ryder had put it out for her. She stood very still for a moment, listening to the quiet sounds of the cabin. Then she began to relax slightly. He wasn't in the house, she was certain now.

A bath, she thought grimly, that was what she needed first. The scent of him seemed to have somehow combined with her own. She made her way to the bathroom and locked the door behind her.

What the hell was the matter with her? Brenna demanded of herself in the mirror. Why was she so nervous this morning? So she had let herself be seduced by a mood and a man unlike any other she had ever known. What was so terrible about that? It wasn't as if she had been unfaithful to Damon. Her relationship with Dr. Fielding hadn't even progressed as far as the bedroom yet and she'd known him, worked with him, for months!

Which didn't make her feel one bit better. Brenna looked away from the anxious expression in her own eyes, turned on the shower, and stepped underneath the spray with alacrity.

No, her relationship with Damon hadn't gotten to the point her association with Ryder Sterne had reached in three days! With a shock of startled realization, Brenna knew that even if she were to know Damon Fielding another ten years, even if she were to go to bed with him every night of that ten years, her relationship with him would never be quite what she'd found with Ryder last night.

The knowledge made her catch her lower lip between her teeth, and another rush of panic seemed to tingle through her bloodstream. Why had she gotten herself into this mess? She closed her eyes at the thought of how Ryder had given her a chance to halt matters before it was too late.

But it had already been too late, even at that point. Somehow the culmination of the evening had been inevitable. Not a pleasant thought for someone who taught the ethics of responsibility and free choice! Brenna's fingers curled into a small fist and she braced her forearm against the tiled wall of the shower. Leaning her forehead against her arm, she let the warm water pound over her while she tried desperately to think.

Over and over again she told herself that nothing all that devastating had happened. She had never been a promiscuous person and she needn't condemn herself for succumbing to the incredible attraction Ryder had held for her last night. There had been very, very few serious romances in her life, she reflected bracingly. Surely a woman her age was allowed the mind-spinning excitement of a night like last night at least once.

She knew, though, that she was, in a sense, chastising herself to no purpose. It wasn't that she felt guilty; it wasn't that she felt as if she'd been disloyal to Damon, who certainly dated other women. There was no point in berating herself for any of the traditional reasons.

The real problem, the one that had to be faced, was that last night had been, in some indefinable way, an act of surrender. She had given herself to Ryder and he had taken possession.

What if he chose to retain that possession now that the night of passion had passed?

With that thought, the full truth surfaced amid the chaos of her thoughts and Brenna straightened away from the shower wall. Facing a truth with intelli-

gence and dispassionate calm was something she was
normally very good at.

Unfortunately the kind of truth she was usually
compelled to face was of an intellectual nature that
made no real impact on her emotions. This was of
an altogether different nature and she swallowed unhappily at the implications.

What was Ryder thinking this morning? Where
was he? Perhaps he would make everything easy for
her by letting the happenings of the night slip away
into oblivion. Perhaps he would make no further demands now that morning had come. He, too, had
been sharing her separate reality last night. With the
advent of day he might have returned, as she had, to
the real world.

But then she remembered the curious, restrained
hunger in him that she had been so eager to unleash
and satisfy. Brenna knew instinctively that it was
more than a physical appetite. She had sensed that
from the beginning. What had she done by giving it
herself to feed upon?

It all came down to an emotion more primitive
than she would have imagined could still exist in a
civilized, intelligent, reasonably sophisticated human
female. She felt claimed.

Unnerved, Brenna turned off the shower and
reached clumsily for one of the thick, striped towels.
Claimed. Possessed.

What if Ryder chose to exercise his claim?

This was ridiculous, Brenna told herself violently
as she furiously towel-dried her dark hair. Utterly
ridiculous! What was the matter with her? Number
one, he probably wouldn't dare presume too much

on the basis of one night, and number two, she was a mature, independent woman who could handle the matter firmly and politely if he did!

Oh, lord! Who was she kidding?

Her scattered thoughts ricocheted around inside her head as she dragged a comb through the wet tendrils of her hair and twisted the dark mass into a long braid that hung down between her shoulders. The severity of the style suited her mood, she thought wretchedly.

Where was Ryder?

Sooner of later she was going to have to deal with the man, she told herself tensely as she pulled on her jeans and found a long-sleeved plaid shirt. She was tucking in the ends of it and groping under the bed for her flat sandals when she heard a knock on the door. Brenna froze.

Blindly she glanced down at the shoe she had retrieved. It wasn't her flat, casual sandal at all. It was the red high-heeled dress shoe Ryder had removed last night. The knock sounded once more, this time with a note of impatience that surprised her.

Why was Ryder knocking in the first place, and in the second, why should he sound impatient? He was the one who had left her bed this morning. Knowing him, she couldn't understand why he didn't feel quite free to walk back into her cabin at his leisure.

"Brenna! Are you inside?"

With a gasp Brenna got to her feet, still clutching the red sandal. The voice outside her door wasn't Ryder's. It belonged to Damon Fielding!

The next knock jolted her into action. As she

started down the stairs she shook her head in annoyance. She had to get a grip on herself.

It should have been harder to open the door to Damon Fielding than it would have been to open it to Ryder. Damon, after all, occupied a much more important role in her life and there was a great deal unsettled between them. He was the man who could assist her in her career, guide her through the intricacies of faculty politics, and lately, she had begun to think, the man whom she might eventually marry. But somehow, when she turned the knob, all Brenna could think of was how grateful she was that she wasn't going to have to face Ryder just yet.

"Damon! What in the world are you doing here?"

She looked up at the dark-haired man of medium height who stood on her doorstep. Professor Damon Fielding had spent a year studying at Oxford sometime in his academic past and it still showed. He wore the tweed jacket with its leather patches on the elbows, the button-down shirt, and the slacks and loafers with aplomb. Nearing forty, Dr. Fielding was aware of his position as next in line to assume the responsibilities of head of the Department of Philosophy when Paul Humphrey retired. He was a good-looking man with stylishly cut hair of the proper length and charmingly blue eyes. He had been divorced from his first wife, a professor of English, for three years. He was, above all else, a highly respected scholar in his area of expertise.

"Good morning, Brenna. Going somewhere exciting?" He smiled down at her and the red sandal she still held in her hand.

"No, no, of course not." Hurriedly Brenna backed

away, gesturing him politely inside. "I'm astonished to see you, Damon. Did you drive all this way just to find me?"

"Who else do I know in Lake Tahoe?" He chuckled, stooping to kiss her lightly. "Got a cup of coffee for a man who's had a long trip?"

"Right away. How about breakfast? Did you stop along the way?" Thankful for the excuse, Brenna hurried toward the kitchen.

"No, and I'll admit that sounds like an excellent suggestion." Damon wandered interestedly into the living room, glancing around. "Enjoying the summer, Brenna?"

"It's hardly started," she protested a little weakly, searching the refrigerator for something edible. It would have to be eggs and toast and coffee. "Did you…did you drive up just for the day?"

"No, I was visiting a colleague in Sacramento and decided on the spur of the moment to come on up to Tahoe. I was a little worried about you, darling."

She glanced up to see him watching her, his hands thrust into the pockets of his jacket. Any moment now he would light his pipe and the image would be complete. Her lips tightened as she closed the refrigerator door.

"It's kind of you to be concerned, Damon," she began formally, "but this is something I'm going to have to think about for a while."

"That's why I'm here, darling," he explained magnanimously, "to help you think. Normally you're one of the most rational, analytical people I know, but on this one subject you can't seem to be realistic."

"Damon, Paul Humphrey is publishing my work under his own name, for God's sake! That's wrong, any way you look at it! Unethical, unprofessional, dishonorable, and unworthy! What the hell do you expect me to do? I may only be a very junior assistant professor but I've got my rights!"

"You also have your future to consider!" he snapped forcefully, clearly annoyed with her inability to be reasonable.

"My future involves teaching things like ethics and the honorable quest for truth! How can I presume to teach such things when I'm personally choosing to ignore them!"

They faced each other across the short space of the kitchen. Where in the world was Ryder? Brenna wondered incongruously. Where had he gone when he'd left her bed this morning? And why was she thinking about him at a time like this? Damon Fielding had come all this way to talk sense into her. She should be thrilled at this sign of his concern!

"Brenna, you're living in the real world, not some perfect construct where everyone behaves according to an ethical code! Be reasonable. Paul Humphrey will be retiring very soon, perhaps even earlier than we thought. His career is over and yours is just beginning. You can't punish him, because it would always be a case of your word against his. He's got a brilliant academic career behind him. You've got virtually nothing yet, except your doctorate and a bottom rung on the faculty ladder. You'll only wind up hurting your own future, perhaps even destroying it, if you accuse him of stealing your work!"

"No wonder you're so good in front of a class full

of students, Damon.'' She tried to smile weakly. ''Your logic is impeccable and your delivery is perfect!'' She pulled out the frying pan and began to crack eggs into a bowl. ''But it's no good. I honestly don't know if I can go back and work for the man in the fall.''

''You little idiot,'' he declared tightly, his temper apparently on edge. With reason, she thought fleetingly. He hadn't even had breakfast yet and here he was trying to deal with a crazy young faculty member. ''You'll be back in the fall and you know it! What else can you do? Jobs for philosophy professors are damn scarce! It could take you months, maybe a year to line up another one. And in the end you would have achieved nothing.''

''How about my pride and self-respect?'' she hazarded dryly, beating the eggs violently.

''What good are they going to do you in a world where there are a lot of Paul Humphreys? And that's the way it will be, Brenna. Our faculty politics are no different than those of any other college or university. If you're going to get ahead, you've got to play the game. That means not embarrassing men like Paul Humphrey or making yourself look like a fool!''

''Good lord, Damon! You make it sound like corporate politics in the business world! All the maneuvering and power struggles and the pains taken to avoid embarrassing the boss or yourself!'' She dropped the egg beater and whirled to face him, her hands on her hips.

''That's exactly what it's like! There's a price on

success in any sphere, and playing the political game is part of that price,'' he grated.

''You're telling me you think it's all right to pay the price?'' she challenged tersely.

''Yes, damn it! It's the only way one can make a contribution to his or her profession!''

''The ends justify the means? Do you realize what you're saying, Damon? We're talking about theft and dishonorable conduct. Do you realize what you're condoning? What that makes you?''

She didn't know why she pushed him that far. She certainly never intended to do so. Perhaps it was because she was so unnerved and upset with herself this morning. Brenna only knew she hadn't meant to enrage the man she had actually been contemplating marrying!

But she had done exactly that. She saw the red flush sweep into his face, saw the hardening line of his mouth, and the next instant his palm connected with the side of her cheek in an instinctive reaction to the insult in her words and eyes.

Even as she flinched automatically from the blow, Damon was being whirled around by the shoulder. Ryder was in the room.

She had never seen him enter, never heard that silent stride as he crossed to the kitchen. The first intimation of his presence was when he swung a fist that collided with Damon's jaw.

Dr. Damon Fielding toppled to the floor before Brenna's horrified gaze.

Five

"Damon!"

Rushing to the fallen man's side was an automatic reflex, Brenna realized even as she did so. She would have gone to the aid of whichever man had taken the fall.

"Leave him alone, Brenna, he'll be fine." Ryder's voice was incredibly soft.

But she was already kneeling on the floor beside the other man even as Damon groaned and opened his eyes weakly. She threw a furious, accusing glare up at Ryder, who stood easily, feet slightly braced, his expression utterly unruffled. He had obviously been back to his own cabin, because he was again wearing the black denim jeans he favored and an open-throated white shirt with a tiny stripe in it. His brown and gold hair was lightly raked by the morning breeze and his recent exertion, and when his sil-

ver-gray eyes met Brenna's angry glance, she saw
the memory of last night hovering just below the
surface. For some reason that fueled her own fury
and disgust.

"There was no call for this kind of violence, Ryder," she stormed. "Is this how you handle any
problem that comes along? With stupid acts of un-
thinking machismo? This man is a colleague of mine!
A respected professor of philosophy! Do you realize
what you've done?"

Ryder looked down at her, his eyes momentarily
unreadable. "He deserved it. He struck you."

"Well, I deserved that!" she raged. "I said some
terrible things to him, insulted him!" And she had,
Brenna thought, horrified. She'd unforgivably insulted the man who had cared enough about her future in the academic world to come all this way to
talk sense to her. Why had she done such a thing?

"Get away from him, Brenna. Come here." Ryder
didn't seem inclined to argue at the moment. His
attention went to his victim, who was slowly lifting
a hand to touch a tender jaw.

Defiantly Brenna didn't move, turning a worried
glance down at Damon. "Damon, Damon, I'm so
sorry about all this! I never meant to insult you like
that and I certainly never meant to involve you in a
fight with Ryder. Are you all right? Here, let me help
you…"

"Brenna, I said get away from him. Come over
here or I'll come and get you."

This time something in his voice reached her and
Brenna tensed. She had heard that soft, gentle tone
before—when he was giving a command and when

he was making love. In both instances, she had discovered, it was equally dangerous. Uncertainly she
got to her feet, her worried eyes still on Damon, who
was painfully sitting up. The other man's attention
was focused narrowly on Ryder.

"Who's the cowboy, Brenna? Friend of yours, I
take it. Is this how you always spend your summers?
Shacked up with some stud you wouldn't normally
be seen with during the academic year?"

"Oh, Damon, please, you don't understand..."
Brenna began plaintively. She heard the enraged hu-
miliation in his words and wanted to soothe it away.
It was all her fault.

"That's enough from both of you," Ryder cut in
dryly. "In case either of you has failed to notice the
fact, I happen to be the one in charge here at the
moment and I'm not in the mood to listen to any
more accusations, apologies, or uncouth comments.
You, Professor, will get to your feet and get out of
here. You're not badly hurt and you know it. If, however, you ever lay another hand on Brenna, I will
personally take you apart, is that quite clear?"

. "Go to hell." But Damon was on his feet and
moving resentfully toward the door. When Brenna
would have put out a placating hand to touch his
sleeve, her face anguished, Ryder stopped her with a
single word.

"Brenna!"

Her hand fell away and she watched the other man
walk out the door. She knew even as she watched
his retreating tweed jacket that it wasn't just a man
walking out of her life, but in all likelihood, her entire future at the college where Damon Fielding

would someday be head of the Department of Philosophy. She hadn't been ready yet to make such a final decision, and now that decision had been made for her. Eyes flaming, she whirled on Ryder as Damon slammed the door.

"Do you have any idea of what you've just done? How did you dare? How could you presume to walk in here this morning and ruin my whole life!"

He stared at her for a moment. "Brenna, I walked in here and found a strange male slapping you around. What the hell did you expect me to do?" She had the feeling he wasn't accustomed to explaining his actions to anyone.

"I would have expected a rational, intelligent, civilized man to ask a few questions and find out what was going on before he interfered!"

He arched an eyebrow. "Okay," he shrugged, "so what was going on?"

"Damn you! It's a little late to be asking that now, isn't it?"

"You mean too late now that I've, uh, ruined your whole life?" he queried wryly.

"It's not a joke!"

"You can say that again! Do you have any idea what it's like for a man to walk in on a scene like the one I just witnessed? My God, Brenna, he's lucky I didn't beat him to a pulp!"

"What stopped you?" she gritted scathingly.

"Chalk it up to the fact that I was feeling magnanimous after spending such a delightful evening," he bit out far too gently. Belatedly it began to occur to Brenna that Ryder was furious.

"A delightful evening enjoying the novelty of seducing a college professor?" she hissed tauntingly.

"A delightful evening being seduced by one," he corrected coolly. "I wasn't the one who rushed matters, as I recall. I distinctly remember saying I was prepared to wait."

"You're saying that last night was my fault?" she blazed, her anger now at such a high level, she had momentarily forgotten Damon.

He considered that. "Yes."

"Why, you ill-bred, ill-mannered, ill-behaved…"

"Stud?" he offered helpfully, a new emotion rousing in the silver eyes to douse some of the controlled fury. Humor?

It was more than Brenna could stand, coming as it did after everything she'd been through in the past twelve hours. She swiveled and grabbed at the nearest object that came to hand, a philosophy text as it happened. Without a pause she sent it sailing toward her tormentor.

The flicker of amusement vanished in Ryder's expression as he stepped aside and let the missile crash into the wall behind him. For an instant after the text had landed harmlessly on the floor, there was utter silence in the room. Brenna stood staring, eyes wide, lips parted in shock at her own violence. And then Ryder started toward her.

Panic overwhelmed her. She wanted to turn and flee but couldn't find the muscle control to do so. The combination of her own guilt, the trauma of the morning's events, and remnants of her anger somehow combined to make it impossible for her to run from him. Since there was no alternative, Brenna stood her ground, hands curled into fists on her hips, chin tilted in a defiance she was far from feeling.

He paced toward her with the gliding, deliberate stride of a hunting cat, and when he reached a point less than a step away he stopped.

"As I've said before, you don't cower when the chips are down, do you?" His words were almost whimsical.

Brenna said nothing; her breath was coming a little too quickly and her pulse was racing, fired by the adrenaline of her emotions.

"Can I take it from your reaction that you don't consider me merely an amusing stud with whom you've decided to shack up this summer?" he persisted dryly.

"You're being insufferable," she managed tightly.

"I know," he admitted on a sigh of regret. "You'll have to forgive me. I've had a trying few minutes."

To her utter astonishment he spun around on one booted heel and started toward the kitchen. "There is a time for action and a time for talk, lady. There is also a time to eat. The action's over and I suggest we proceed to the other two items on the agenda. Ah, good, you've already started," he added calmly as he plucked another egg out of the carton.

Driven by an impulse she didn't quite understand, Brenna narrowed her eyes and said meaningfully, "I was fixing breakfast for Damon."

"Damon's gone," he pointed out blandly.

"Ryder..."

"Sit down, Brenna. We're going to talk."

The underlying steel in the too-gentle voice was

enough to convince her to do as he said. He wasn't the only one who'd had a trying few minutes. Mutely she crossed slowly to the round wooden table near the window and sank into the chair, watching as he methodically fixed breakfast.

He took in the sight of her tightly folded hands and stiff shoulders and the silent resentment in her eyes and shook his head once before he went back to cracking eggs. "I'm not going to apologize for what just happened, Brenna. Any man who walked in on a scene like that would have reacted in the same manner."

"Any man who makes it a habit to indulge his physical, violent reactions to a situation, you mean!"

He lifted one shoulder dismissingly. "If you think that was bad, you ought to see what I would have done if I'd walked in and found him kissing you, instead! Besides, if I may take the liberty of saying so, the man was engaging in a little violence himself!"

Brenna squeezed her eyes shut in pained memory and seemed to sag a little in despair. "Oh, Ryder, you should have heard what I said to him!"

"I did hear some of it but I didn't understand it all. What was going on, Brenna?" he prompted quietly as he poured tea.

She looked up at him bleakly. "The man came up here to help me. He's concerned about me, my career. I'm…I'm in the middle of a major decision, you see. Whatever I decide to do will affect my whole future. Poor Damon was only trying to make me see the reasonable side of the situation…" She gave a muffled exclamation and reached for the tea he had poured. "Never mind, it's complicated and I doubt that you'd really be interested—"

"You know damn well I'm interested," he interrupted grimly. "Go on."

Brenna hesitated a moment longer and then gave in. What did it matter if she told him the tale? "You must have heard how it is in the academic world when it comes to the importance of faculty members getting published in their field?"

"Publish or perish?"

"I'm afraid it truly is that bad. If you want to advance and gain tenure, it's an absolute necessity. I have been working for months on a major paper on the subject of computer ethics…"

"Computer ethics!" Ryder appeared startled for the first time.

Brenna smiled a tiny, wan smile. "It's a hot new field for philosophy as a whole. Practically speaking, philosophy departments have fallen out of favor on a lot of campuses. Not everyone still sees the study of philosophy as critical to a modern education. The issue of the ethics of computer use and abuse in the modern world is a way for philosophy to get back into the mainstream and help keep itself alive as an intellectual field. It's kind of an *applied* philosophy." She paused and looked at him uncertainly.

"Okay, I'll take your word for it," he muttered, peering closely at the scrambled eggs in the frying pan.

"At any rate, I've put a lot of work into a paper that assesses the logic and ethics of computers in the light of historical philosophical thinking. Relating what people like Aristotle and Kant and others have written to the modern problem of computer use is fascinating, Ryder. It provides all sorts of new insights, opens up all kinds of questions…'' For a few seconds the enthusiasm she felt for her subject wiped out the dull anxiety in her amber eyes.

Ryder half smiled. ''Again, I'll take your word for it.''

Brenna gave herself a slight mental shake and returned to the main issue. ''I had a lot of notes and a rough outline of what I wanted to say in my office. It was no secret that I was preparing the paper in order to submit it to a major journal in the field. One weekend I went into my office on a Sunday, which is something I rarely do. I had intended to put a little extra time in on the project. When I arrived, the whole file of my notes and the outline were gone.''

''Stolen?'' he demanded, obviously intrigued by the turn of events.

''They were back in my desk drawer on Monday morning,'' she told him flatly. ''I couldn't figure out what in the world was going on. I got paranoid and started taking the file home with me, but by then the damage had already been done. Lord only knows how many Sundays the file had spent out of my desk and on someone else's!''

''Whose?''

''The head of my department, that's who!'' Brenna proclaimed with renewed anger. ''The eminent Dr. Paul Humphrey, who wanted to mark his last year in the academic world with a paper that would give the impression that he was at the forefront of modern philosophy! I suppose I should be flattered," she added disparagingly. "I didn't know the work I'd done was *that* good!"

"How did you find out?"

"It was announced this past week that a major monograph written by him had been submitted and accepted for publication in an important philosophical journal. Copies of the monograph were passed around so that the faculty could read and admire the work of their department chief. I hadn't finished the first page before I realized I was reading my own research and analysis!"

"So you stood up at the next faculty party and accused your boss of being a thief?" Ryder asked interestedly as he served up the eggs and toast and sat down across from Brenna. "Must have been a sight worth seeing."

"I did not make any open accusations. I was in a quandary so I went to the person I felt closest to on the faculty, the man who will very possibly be the next department head..."

"The man I just kicked out the front door?"

"His name is Damon Fielding. Dr. Damon Fielding," she emphasized through clenched teeth.

"And he immediately took up cudgels on your behalf?" Ryder hazarded coolly, chewing on a slice of whole wheat toast.

Brenna sighed. "He sympathized; said he believed me but there was nothing either of us could do about it. Humphrey is a law unto himself, he said, and I would only get hurt if I tried to challenge the man over an issue like this. He's a well-known established scholar and I'm just a beginner. He tried to impress upon me the fact that if I'm going to succeed in my chosen profession, I've got to learn to play the politics of the situation. He…he made it sound as if we were out in the corporate world with all its nasty infighting and games on the way to the top.''

"He's probably right,'' Ryder surprised her by saying readily.

She blinked at him owlishly, not having expected quite that reaction.

"Any situation in which there's a lot of competition for the top rung of a ladder is going to create a climate of that sort. It's true in the military world, the corporate world, and, I'm sure, in the academic world. You can't change that fact of life, lady, all you can do is decide whether or not you're going to play the game. The thing to remember is that the choice is yours.''

"You seem to have given the matter some thought,'' she said thinly.

"Sure, I've faced the situation before. That's one of the reasons I've done some of the things I've done and one of the reasons I'm writing adventure fiction. I made the choice of living life on my own terms as much as possible. This is the way I do that,'' he concluded simply.

Brenna stared at him in consternation and then asked the question that was uppermost in her mind. "What would you have done if you'd been Damon?'' she breathed.

He gave her a steady glance. "You mean if you'd come to me with proof that the head of the department had stolen your material? Something ill-bred, ill-mannered, and ill-behaved, no doubt. Also something violent. Lady, I would have fought on your behalf and in the process probably gotten us both kicked out of the college,'' Ryder told her bluntly. ''All of which is not to say that my way is any better or worse than your friend Damon's. In the end you're the one who has to make the decision.''

''Yes.'' She nodded, acknowledging the inescapable truth. ''Although it looks as though I've already made it. Damon won't forgive that little scene this morning. And it was all my fault; I should never have precipitated it by pointing out to him that he was condoning unethical and disreputable behavior by not speaking up on my behalf.''

''That's the comment that made him lose his temper and slap you?''

She nodded. ''I insulted him terribly when you think about it. He was only trying to help me. He came all this way to help me, in fact.''

''Exactly how much does the man mean to you?'' Ryder demanded with sudden intensity. ''I'm getting the impression he's more than merely a colleague.''

''He is…was…'' Brenna lifted a hand vaguely. ''We were quite close. We date regularly and…'' She couldn't quite meet the piercing silver eyes now.

''And you were thinking of a more permanent arrangement?'' Ryder growled.

''I thought we were rather well matched, as a matter of fact. We respect each other, enjoy each other's company, have an enormous amount in common…'' she began belligerently.

''None of which means anything after last night,'' he broke in to say in a very even tone. ''And don't look at me as if you're experiencing total shock. You don't have all that much in common with Damon

Fielding or you wouldn't have been so hurt by his failure to champion your cause. If you'd had so much in common, you would have known him well enough to predict exactly how he'd react in the situation you described. On the other hand," he added imperturbably, "you knew me well enough after only three days to be not at all surprised at how I reacted to that little scene this morning!"

"What are you talking about?" She glowered at him, her stomach tensing with premonition.

"Whatever you had with Fielding is over," he explained calmly. "You made that decision last night when you invited me into your bed. I warned you I'd hold you to your choice once you made it. You belong to me now, Brenna Llewellyn."

You belong to me. The words hammered into her mind as she sat staring at the man sitting across the table from her. "No," she whispered desperately. "No, you don't understand…"

"Are you going to try running away?" he asked as if only academically interested in the answer. Ryder reached for another slice of toast.

"If you think we have so much in common that we can predict each other's reactions, you tell me!" she shot back furiously. How dare he sit there so calmly and talk about her *belonging* to him? Maybe in his world people thought in such primitive terms, but certainly not in hers! But she had known ever since she awoke this morning that this was coming. It was the wrongness she'd been aware of since she'd opened her eyes. She had known she'd made a tremendous mistake letting herself be swept away by the mood of the evening. How could she have been so incredibly *stupid?*

He was chewing his toast and contemplating her question. ''To tell you the truth I can see you going either way,'' he finally stated with a nod. ''You might run just to see if I really will come after you.''

''That would be childish in the extreme!'' she snapped, incensed because the question had leaped into her mind the moment he had suggested the fact that she might actually choose to run away. Would he come after her? It was useless to speculate. Brenna Llewellyn didn't resort to such emotional tricks. She had been trained to deal with problems much more intelligently than that!

''Not childish, but perhaps tritely feminine,'' he corrected judiciously. ''To save you the bother, I'll tell you right now that I would, indeed, come after you. And I probably wouldn't be in the best of moods when I found you, either. But if I had to bet on the most likely reaction, my money would be on the side that says you'll stay and battle this out even though the conclusion is a foregone one after last night.''

''Hardly!''

One tawny brow arched in cool mockery. ''The conclusion *is* foregone, lady, but if it will soothe your frazzled nerves I'll reassure you that I'm still willing to wait. Just as I was willing to wait last night. I won't push you back into bed.''

''You're too generous!'' Brenna couldn't believe what she was hearing. The morning was shaping up disastrously!

The brackets at the edge of his mouth softened

although he didn't quite smile. "It's not a question of generosity, Brenna. It's just that I know you well enough to realize that what happened last night happened a little too soon. I knew it at the time but I did warn you that I'd hold you to your decision. This morning you're feeling panicked and unnerved and I'd just as soon you didn't run away from me, so I'm giving you the time you need to settle everything in your own head to your satisfaction. There are obviously some other major decisions awaiting you in regard to your career. You've clearly got enough on your mind without having to worry about what you'll do if I try to carry you off to bed."

"You're so damn sure of yourself," she whispered incredulously.

"It's not me I'm sure of, it's you. You're a woman of honor—I know you won't be able to turn your back on what happened between us last night. You only need a little time to deal with it. Don't panic, lady, I'm a very patient man when the goal is this important," he concluded kindly.

Brenna swallowed, stricken. "Aren't you reading a great deal into one rather reckless night?"

He did smile this time, memories dancing in his eyes. "It was reckless, wasn't it? All things considered, you're turning out to have quite a streak of recklessness in your makeup. Did you know that about yourself before this summer?"

For some reason tears began to threaten behind Brenna's amber eyes. It was all too much. She didn't know how to cope with everything happening at once like this: the crisis in her career; the crisis with this man. He was right about one thing, she thought wretchedly, she did need time. Brenna got to her feet in a quick, convulsive movement, her hands gripping the edge of the table. "If you'll excuse me," she began very formally, striving to conquer the tears, "I'm going to take a walk. It's been a difficult morning." She turned half blindly and left the cabin.

Half an hour later she sat, knees drawn up and arms resting on top of them, and gazed out over the crystal-blue lake. She had found the small private cove a short distance from the cabin and it was exactly the place she needed. The tears had never actually fallen, to her vast relief. They had been a product of frustration and panic, and she was proud to have resisted the impulse to cry for such reasons. She could handle her life successfully without resorting to tears. Hadn't she always managed to do so?

But she needed to think and so far she hadn't gotten very far with the process. She still felt too on edge, too hemmed in, and a little frightened. The thought of calling her brother occurred briefly and was immediately dismissed. There was nothing he could do and a full explanation of the situation would only anger him. That thought brought a wry twist to her mouth. He wasn't altogether unlike Ryder in his reactions. He'd come out of the corner fighting on her behalf even though this was clearly a case where violence was not very useful. It never was, she reminded herself staunchly.

A faint warning tingle made her glance up sharply to see Ryder emerging on catlike feet from the pines behind her. He was carrying a couple of books and a thermos.

"It's a perfect day to sit and read by the lake with

a cup of hot tea, isn't it?'' he inquired conversation-
ally, sinking down beside her with a masculine grace
that stirred up images of last night in her mind. The
silver eyes met hers with a measure of understanding
and reassurance.

"Ryder, I don't—"

"I brought you a book," he interrupted quietly,
unscrewing the cap of the thermos.

Automatically she glanced down at the two volumes resting on his lap. One was the philosophy text
she had thrown at him and the other was one of his
own adventure tales, complete with lurid cover.

"Thanks," she told him stiffly, "but I'm not in
the mood to study philosophy at the moment."

"I brought the philosophy book for me to read,"
he murmured, handing her a mug of tea. "I brought
the other book for you."

Their eyes locked as his meaning registered. "You
want me to read one of your stories?"

"I know the stuff isn't exactly your taste in fiction,
and I know I'm not the most brilliant of authors, but
I would like you to read one of my books. Will
you?"

"Why?" she heard herself ask huskily, picking up
the paperback in his lap and examining it curiously.

"Because there's something of me in my books
and you're an intelligent woman. You'll find it.
Maybe in the process you'll learn something about
me."

She felt dazed, taken totally off guard. "And
you're going to tackle that book of philosophical
readings?"

"I'm interested in finding out more about what

you do for a living,'' he answered smilingly, leaning back against the large boulder behind him and opening the textbook.

''There's no point in this exercise,'' she protested halfheartedly, focusing on the cover of the paperback. ''We're totally unlike, Ryder. What are you hoping to accomplish?''

''I've told you, a little mutual understanding. I think it's important since we're going to be living together,'' he added, already flipping through the introductory pages of the book and studying the table of contents.

''Living together! Are you crazy? Ryder, last night was a mistake, you must see that!''

''Why?'' he asked simply, lifting his head to study her earnest face.

''Because you're assuming far too much from what happened!''

The silvery gaze moved over her. ''The night you came sneaking through my window I knew I wanted you. Last night you proved you want me.''

''That's not sufficient grounds on which to make a decision like living together,'' she got out huskily. The tension his words generated in her was frightening. A part of her longed to agree with him, to surrender herself to the summer and to him.

''We also happen to need each other, lady,'' he told her coolly.

''How can you say that? We hardly even know each other,'' she exploded.

''I can't explain it completely, not yet. I don't have all the right words. But I'm sure of the feeling. Maybe that's why I want you to read my book. Perhaps I'm hoping you'll understand something of what I'm trying to say.''

She felt helpless in the face of the quiet plea. She was right, of course, there was no point to the exercise, but she didn't know how to refuse him. Brenna glanced down again at the paperback he had given her.

''What if this doesn't work? What if I'm still of the same opinion after I finish the book as I am now?''

''I don't think you've got any clear-cut opinions right now.'' He chuckled. ''You're much too mixed up at the moment to be thinking with any great clarity.''

''Hardly a good time to be studying your character through your stories,'' she retorted, knowing already that she was going to do as he asked and read the book.

''I'll take my chances.''

''Maybe you're the one who will be put off by my character when you get into that long, dry book of philosophy readings!'' she challenged, settling back against the same sun-warmed rock he was leaning on. ''Have you thought about that? You're likely to realize I'm merely a dull, staid, unapproachable teacher of a subject that never interested you much in the first place.''

''Is that how you see yourself?'' he asked in amusement.

Her mouth turned downward a little ruefully. ''To tell you the truth, I've never thought of myself or my profession as dull and unapproachable, but I'm fully aware that others might see both that way.''

"There's not much this book could do to change the image I already have of you, lady." Ryder grinned. "It's just going to give me a little more complete view, that's all."

Brenna hesitated, wanting to ask him exactly how he did see her but not quite having the nerve. Instead she said casually, "Ryder, about last night..."

He leaned forward and stopped her words by the simple expedient of sealing her mouth with a slow kiss. It was a lingering, tasting caress that spoke of remembered ecstasy and satisfaction. It spoke of satiated hunger that could be roused again with very little provocation. Brenna stayed quite still beneath the impact of it, finding it strangely soothing after the chaos of the morning.

"Let's not spoil last night with any more words, sweet lady," he growled, lifting his head with obvious reluctance.

Fingers trembling very faintly, Brenna picked up the paperback novel in her lap.

Six

It was called *The Quicksilver Venture* and the cover guaranteed it to be another tale of action and intrigue by Justin Murdock. The artwork featured the predictably lusty, well-muscled hero, menaced apparently by an assortment of cobras. The beautiful woman sprawled in terror at his feet was a redhead this time, and while the pose was decidedly sensual, Brenna had the impression that the manner in which she was clinging to the hero's ankle was hampering his attempt to defend them both from the cobras. He was armed only with a thin-bladed knife.

Not quite certain why she had let herself be talked into reading the paperback when, by rights, she should have been trying to sort out the growing confusion of her career and her relationship with Damon Fielding, Brenna turned the page and began to read. Perhaps it was a form of procrastination, she told herself fleetingly. Things were happening in her life, forcing choices upon her that she really didn't want to face. Reading *The Quicksilver Venture* was a way of avoiding the facts. Or was it? she wondered as she began to read.

He was good, I had to admit, but he was probably still new to the business. He didn't make allowances for either the age of the old hotel window or for the fact that agents who have stayed alive as long as I have tend to sleep a little differently than people who have nice, normal, routine jobs. Then, again, perhaps I was still half awake because of the dream about the blonde in Paris. Whatever the reason, I heard the faint creak and I didn't spend any time telling myself it was the normal sort of sound one expected to hear in a venerable English inn. My hand under the pillow closed around the handle of the stiletto.

I didn't move as he slipped silently into the room. Then I sensed my uninvited guest taking that quiet, mind-steadying breath you need when you're aiming a gun at a target shrouded in shadows and you know you'll only get one chance.

The stiletto left my hand in the same instant I dove for the floor on the opposite side of the bed. Sensing disaster, my visitor fired, but the muffled shot went wild because the long, thin blade that had become an extension of my fingers over the years was already burying itself in his throat. Like the silenced automatic, his scream was also muffled.

I picked myself up off the floor and flipped on the overhead light with a sigh of regret. It was, all in all, a hell of a way to start a vacation.

In spite of herself, Brenna experienced a flicker of wry amusement at the memory of how she had awakened Ryder that first night. Then the amusement faded rather abruptly. Perhaps she'd been rather lucky!

The action-packed tale moved quickly. By the end of the first chapter the hero, one Hunt Cameron, found himself immersed in a dangerous mission to bring a defector known only as Quicksilver out of Eastern Europe. But the relatively straightforward adventure was given a few twists. Cameron was assigned to work with a beautiful new agent, Cassandra Vaughn, who, Brenna presumed, was the redhead on the cover. Cassandra, apparently, was from a modern, technologically sophisticated school of espionage. She was highly skilled in computer-assisted analysis techniques, used the latest in communications gadgets, and was trained to work by the book. Quicksilver was to be her first mission.

Hunt Cameron, on the other hand, had thrown out the book years ago in order to stay alive in the field. He relied on such unscientific things as hunches, well-developed instincts, and a very non-routine way of handling matters. The only tool in which he put any trust was the stiletto he carried always, even to bed. He didn't bother to take the risk of trusting people. Hunt and Cass clashed from the moment they met.

Underlying the conflict between the admittedly chauvinistic professional and the lovely, disdainful beginner was, of course, an undeniable physical attraction. Of course. Brenna found herself reading the love scenes with great attention.

At lunchtime she and Ryder, by quiet agreement, went back to his cabin for a sandwich and more tea. They ate in near silence, and Brenna was conscious of a certain restlessness to finish the story. Ryder eyed her obliquely but made no move to detain her. Within half an hour they were both back at the cove, immersed in their reading.

Out on the shimmering lake the occasional outboard roared past. The sun gleamed on the cold water. It was a peaceful mountain setting and Brenna read the remainder of *The Quicksilver Venture* without interruption. She was aware of Ryder beside her, seemingly engrossed in the book of philosophy readings, but all her attention was on the breakneck pace of the paperback adventure in her hands.

When she finally closed the book on the last page late that afternoon, she had to admit that Justin Murdock had given his readers their money's worth. She wondered how many would realize he'd given them something more, too.

"Finished?" Ryder asked softly, closing his own book.

Brenna nodded, her chin resting on her folded arms, which were, in turn, propped on her drawn-up knees. She stared thoughtfully across at the opposite side of the lake. "You tell a great adventure tale,

Ryder, but you've probably been told that any number of times.''

''I like hearing it from you,'' he admitted. She wasn't looking at him but she could feel the faint smile.

There was a short silence and she knew he was waiting for her to go on. ''Lots of violence in the story,'' she mused, knowing she was stepping around the main issue.

''There are certain conventions to be followed in writing that kind of tale,'' he pointed out dryly. Brenna sensed he was well aware that she was going to have to take her time working up to the important aspects.

''Are the love scenes part of the 'conventions'?'' she heard herself ask and immediately could have bitten out her tongue. She sat very stiffly as she awaited his response.

''They aren't love scenes,'' Ryder murmured. ''They're sex scenes. And, yes, they're one of the things the reader expects. I told you once I'm selling sex along with the violence and intrigue.''

Her head swung around sharply as she turned to stare at him. ''But they *were* love scenes!'' she protested.

''Why do you say that?'' he asked blandly, but there was a flicker of hungry curiosity deep in the silver gaze as he watched her frowning features.

''Because, aside from wanting each other, Hunt and Cass learn during the course of the story that they need each other. What they have together isn't just sex, Ryder. Good lord! Why am I telling you that? You're the one who wrote the scenes!''

"Go on," he urged. "I'm fascinated to hear the way a professor of philosophy analyzes a sleazy pulp novel. How can you say the sexy parts were love scenes, though? Never once during the whole course of the story does Hunt tell Cass he loves her."

"And she never gets around to telling him that she loves him, either," Brenna finished on a note of complaint. "You could have put that in on the last page, Ryder. I mean, it was obvious they were deeply in love by the end of the book, anyhow."

"There was nothing mushy or sloppily sentimental about how they felt toward each other."

"You think love is sloppy and sentimental?" she queried, aware of a sense of disappointment.

"My readers would!" he retorted with great conviction.

Brenna laughed at that and turned back to look at the lake as she contemplated another thought. "I like the ending," she finally said simply. "I liked the fact that they both realized they wanted something else out of life and had the courage to go looking for it." Hunt and Cass had both decided to get out of the hard, dangerous profession they had chosen. At the conclusion of the story they had mutually agreed to quietly resign and find another life for themselves, one they could build together.

"You didn't find Cameron too much of a male chauvinist?" Ryder taunted gently.

"Well, strictly speaking, he certainly was in many respects," Brenna said. "I mean, he was always stepping in to handle the rough stuff because he didn't trust Cass to be able to do it. No, I take that back. He stepped in to do the bloody work because he didn't *want* her to have to do it. He simply used his lack of trust in her commando training as an excuse. He was trying to protect her from finding out how devastating it can be to kill another human being, wasn't he? And to shield her from danger.''

"Yes." Ryder spoke the single word very softly.

"Definitely a male chauvinist. He was also aggressive, cynical, ruthless, and dangerous. But I liked him,'' Brenna whispered, staring very hard now at the opposite shore. ''I would have trusted him to the ends of the earth. He was a man of honor and integrity, even if he did make his own rules. Or perhaps he was that way *because* he made them,'' she added with a sense of wonder. ''How much of yourself did you put into Hunt Cameron, Ryder?'' she asked very steadily.

''Beats me,'' he retorted smoothly. ''I think I'll leave that for you to decide.

She didn't look at him as she mulled that over. In her trained, analytical brain some unavoidable conclusions were beginning to form. Brenna wasn't at all sure she liked them.

They revolved around the fact that she really had wound up admiring Hunt Cameron and the code he lived by. Like Cass in the story, she found herself attracted to the strength and integrity in the man even though she periodically became thoroughly irritated with his methods and manners. And Brenna was honest enough with herself to realize that her feelings for Ryder were in danger of paralleling those of the heroine in *Quicksilver* for the hero. The knowledge was frightening. It washed over Brenna like a cold wave and automatically she raised the first defense she could find.

"You didn't have to hit Damon this morning!"

As if he could read her mind, he followed the non sequitur immediately. "You belong to me now, Brenna. There's no way on earth I could let another man get away with striking you. He's lucky I didn't kill him."

Brenna absorbed the impact of the quiet, forceful statement, knowing the truth behind it. Ryder lived by his own code. He felt she had given herself to him last night and he would protect what was his. But, as with Cass in *The Quicksilver Venture*, Brenna felt a need to protest his autocratic assumptions. Ryder was not the right man for her! She needed and wanted someone like Damon Fielding...

But she knew even as she repeated the words to herself that the reason she had hurled accusations at Fielding that morning was precisely because he had fallen far short of her ideal. She had wanted him to defend and protect her in an uncompromising manner.

It wasn't that she wouldn't or couldn't take a stand on her own behalf. Brenna knew she was fully capable of defending herself. But an undeniable part of her had wanted the man she was contemplating marrying to prove himself totally on her side when the going got rough. She had wanted to know that she was the most important thing in his life and that he would not make compromises when it came to protecting her.

All of which was totally unfair, she reasoned deliberately. Damon had tried to protect her in his own way. He had logically advised her to think of her career and her future first, rather than the injustice of the moment. His method was the right approach.

But Ryder would have gone to war for her.

And gotten them both kicked out of the college, Brenna reminded herself ruefully.

On the other hand, something in her knew the line had to be drawn somewhere. Logical compromise was all well and good, but each individual had to decide just how far he or she would go before saying that the limit had been reached. In that moment of self-understanding and analysis, Brenna acknowledged that Damon would go a great deal further than she would when it came to compromising for the sake of a career. How much further?

Before she could explore that question, though, another matter had to be dealt with. Talk about drawing the line somewhere! She was most definitely going to have to do exactly that with Ryder Sterne. Every instinct warned that the attraction she felt for this man was dangerous in the extreme. She realized now, after having read *The Quicksilver Venture,* that his appeal was all the more hazardous because it wasn't simply physical. A very elemental part of her sought the straightforward, utterly unyielding, fiercely independent strength in him. But it was all wrong to find those qualities in this man! She dared not let herself admit that she could give herself completely to a man who was not of the intellectual and academically sophisticated world in which she lived. She had worked so hard gaining entrance to that particular world! It was a kind of heresy to even contemplate the notion that she could fall in love with someone who did not share it with her.

Fall in love! No! Brenna's chin lifted and her amber eyes flared gold as she turned her head to fix Ryder with a condemning stare.

"I do not belong to you, Ryder. Not in any sense of the word. We…we only went to bed together last night, we didn't pledge our love, for heaven's sake!"

He put down the thick philosophy text and leaned forward to capture her face between his palms. The silver in his eyes was a banked flame. Brenna sensed impatience and an equal determination to control that impatience radiating through the lean, hard body.

"I, like my readers, am not interested in sloppy, sentimental words such as 'love.' Please don't use them to cloud the issue. We want each other, Brenna, and we need each other!"

"How can you say that?" she pleaded. "We don't *need* each other! Not in any meaningful way!" But she heard the lie in her own words and was desperately afraid he would see it. A part of her *did* need him; needed his honor and passionate way of living by his own code.

He studied her face searchingly. "Lady, I have spent the day reading the works of the men and women you admire. Shall I tell you what I've learned?" Ryder didn't wait for the answer. "You are a member of a profession that is not afraid to ask questions. The most incredible questions! The questions your predecessors have asked were so fundamental that they literally opened up the areas of human knowledge. They are the questions that are the foundation of science and mathematics and ethics and communications and logic. My God, woman! If you are going to follow in the footsteps of such people, surely you must find the courage to ask a few personal questions of yourself!''

"Such as?" she challenged tightly, her pulse racing as she met the will and the power in him.

"Such as what you want out of life! Such as what you want out of a relationship. Such as what you need from a man and what you're capable of giving in return." His voice deepened, becoming as deceptively soft and gentle as silk. "Such as why you made the decision to invite me into your bed last night."

"I didn't! I..." Brenna closed her eyes against the accusation she sensed in him. "All right, so I did. That's all there was to it, Ryder. I don't know what it is you want from me!"

"You," he told her gently. "All of you. And I want exclusive rights. If I ever find your precious Dr. Fielding touching you again I'll take him apart. I mean it, Brenna. I warned you last night that when you gave yourself to me it would be completely."

"You can't blame me for not understanding how...how completely you meant!" she argued, aware even in frustration and anger how much her body longed to call off the battle. It would be so blissful to simply go into his arms and forget the past and the future. But the need to resist his challenge was just as strong. Brenna knew better than to succumb to the repressed streak of recklessness in her own nature. She could not trust that side of herself; she was sure it would lead to disaster.

"Don't pretend you misunderstood me," he admonished with a wry quirk to his lips, his features softening. "I just finished the chapter on the philosophy of linguistic analysis! Even if I hadn't read it, I would still, as a writer, have a great respect for the power of language, lady. And I know my words last night were very direct and to the point."

"This isn't a joke, Ryder," she protested, sensing the flash of humor in him. "You're trying to push me into a full-scale affair and I won't be driven like that!"

He shook his head once in denial. "I'm not pushing, Brenna. I keep telling you I'm willing to wait."

"You say that and then turn around and make all sorts of demands!"

"You gave me the right to place those demands," he said evenly.

"No!"

"What are you going to do? If you choose to run, I think you know by now that I'll come after you. If you stay here and work things out, I'll give you some time in which to come to terms with yourself and the situation. Take your choice."

Anger surged to life in Brenna. In part it was directed against herself for even being tempted by this man, but she aimed it at him, nonetheless. With a swift movement she pulled herself free of his hands and leaped to her feet, the tension in her stiffening every line of her body.

"How dare you presume to give me such choices, Ryder Sterne! No one, especially no man, has that right! I'll do as I damn well please and I sure as hell don't intend to let myself get boxed into a corner by you. Your conceit and arrogance are amazing! Do you really think I'll let myself be used by you for an affair this summer? Someone to provide a little light relief after a hard day's writing?''

At her words his jaw tightened and his silver eyes became narrow and assessing. Brenna knew she was running a risk but she couldn't seem to stop. She was feeling trapped both by the events of the morning and by the bonds Ryder was attempting to place on her. Her instincts were telling her to fight while there was still some chance of freeing herself. But when Ryder got almost lazily to his feet to stand in front of her, another instinct jerked into awareness. This one instructed her to be prepared to run.

''You know damn good and well that I'm not looking for a 'little light relief,' as you put it,'' he stated coolly. ''If I were, I wouldn't have told you that I was willing to wait politely for another invitation to your bed. Use your head, lady, and stop looking for flimsy excuses to attack me.''

''What sort of excuse should I look for?'' she tossed back flippantly. ''Something tells me you'll label all my excuses flimsy!''

''Oh, you've got some good grounds for being afraid of me at this point,'' he drawled dangerously. ''I represent a threat to your whole way of life.''

''The only threat in my life right now is the one to my career!''

''You're wrong, Brenna. That's the easy one to handle. I'm another kind of threat altogether and you're going to find me a lot tougher to deal with.''

''You're beginning to sound like the character in your novel,'' she spat furiously. Her temper was raging and she didn't seem to be able to bring it under control. Too much had happened to her today, and somehow Ryder seemed the focus of all the problems she faced.

"Maybe you've got it all backward. Perhaps he's the one who sounds like me," Ryder taunted softly.

"Well, I'm not the sexy, beautiful redhead in *The Quicksilver Venture!* I don't intend to let myself be swept off my feet by a tough-talking macho type who thinks that because he wants a woman she should immediately surrender herself, body and soul!"

The only response to that was a casually raised eyebrow. It had the horrifying effect of bringing a warm flush into Brenna's face. She already *had* surrendered herself once. How could she deny it? Brenna drew herself very straight, her head lifted proudly.

"I can see there's not much point in continuing this discussion. If you'll excuse me, I'm going back to the cabin. It's been one hell of an interesting day, I assure you!"

Whirling in the sand, Brenna started for the safety of the pines and her own cabin. She refused to give in to the inclination to run. Not for the world would she allow him to think she was afraid of him! At twenty-nine she was not about to admit to fear of any man. Disgust, disdain, and irritation, perhaps, but not fear!

"Brenna."

Her name was the quiet, snaking coil of a whip. It spun through the air behind her, reaching out and circling to bind her as it settled about her body with almost tangible force. Brenna wanted to run from it but she knew she couldn't. Slowly she halted and turned to face the man who had managed to make the single word a command.

For a long, tense moment they stood staring across the distance between them, each one assessing the other. Brenna felt the palms of her hands grow damp with the force of the conflicting emotions coursing through her.

"Don't give me orders, Ryder."

"I haven't issued any orders. I only called your name," he said quietly.

But it had been an order and they both knew it; one she couldn't deny because it demanded that she have the courage to stand and deal with the threat and the challenge in him.

Without a word he started toward her slowly. "Don't be afraid of me," he growled deeply. "Don't be afraid of yourself."

She watched him come closer and wished she could run. But she couldn't, and there was no point thinking about it. "Ryder, I won't let you seduce me," she whispered.

"No," he agreed, halting a pace away.

She tried again. "I'm...I'm sorry about what happened last night, about the way you interpreted it."

"I'm not."

"Please, don't tease me!"

"No," he agreed again.

"Are you angry?"

"A little provoked," he temporized dryly.

Brenna lifted a hand, feeling helpless. "What are you going to do?"

"Keep pressing my claim until you acknowledge it," he told her calmly.

"Is that a threat?"

"No threats. I won't be back in your bed until you invite me."

Surely that was safe enough, Brenna told herself. She could trust this man. With that thought came another, more impulsive one. She felt compelled to tell him that last night had meant something to her even though she didn't want to be bound by the commitment he was invoking. It was an incredibly difficult thing to say, Brenna discovered.

"Ryder, about last night…"

"Let the subject of last night rest," he said tersely.

"Why?" she demanded in sudden annoyance. "Because we can't agree on what it meant?"

"You know what it meant. You just don't want to admit it. Not yet."

"But you think I will in time?" she challenged.

"We'd better let that subject rest, too." He held out his hand. "Would you like to come over to my place for a sundown drink, dinner, and a little philosophical conversation?" He smiled in whimsical invitation.

She hesitated suspiciously, knowing she was longing to accept the offered hand. The longing and the wariness in her were creating an unbearable tension, she realized. Her fingers quivered slightly as she slowly accepted his hand in a small surrender.

"All right, Ryder. Thank you." There was a sense of relief in the way his fingers closed warmly around hers. She took a steadying breath and then declared, unable to resist, "I still say you should never have struck Damon. Violence is never the answer!"

A slow grin sliced across his tanned features, a

knife blade of a grin. "I disagree. It can be satisfyingly decisive at times! You must occasionally crave for something decisive in your life after dealing with all those endless questions of philosophy."

He started back toward the cabins with her in tow, ignoring her withering glance. "What are you going to do about your job situation?" he asked after a moment.

"I don't know. I honestly don't know. Damon is very influential. He's sure to be next in line for the position of head of the department. After the way I insulted him this morning, I can probably assume I've burned my bridges at the college." Brenna caught her lower lip between her teeth as she considered that. What a mess. The worst of it was that she couldn't determine how she felt about it.

"My decking him probably didn't aid your cause any," Ryder muttered laconically. "Will he fire you or get you fired?"

"I don't think he could do that but..." She let the sentence trail off.

"But he could make life difficult for you on the faculty, right?"

It was the truth. "Yes."

There was a small pause while Ryder appeared to be searching for the words he wanted. "The important thing is that you don't really love him, Brenna," he finally announced forcefully.

"You think love is a sloppy, sentimental emotion, remember? Since you don't have much respect for it yourself, you're hardly in a position to tell me whether or not I'm in love!"

"Take my word for it," he retorted sardonically.

"You're not in love with Damon Fielding. You would never have gone to bed with me last night if you loved him!"

Brenna shook her head, abandoning what was sure to be a fruitless argument. Ryder was too certain of himself and of her. As for herself, Brenna couldn't seem to view her feelings toward Damon with any objectivity today. Ryder had occupied her thoughts from the moment she'd awakened in the empty bed, and it was Ryder who had set the pace for the strange day.

It was easier during this time of uncertainty about her future to simply put the whole subject out of her mind and let Ryder continue to guide the evening. It was, she admitted privately, an unusual way for her to behave. Brenna Llewellyn couldn't even remember the last time in her life when she had allowed someone else to direct the course of events. She had known where she was going, been aware of her responsibilities, and felt the obligations of her duty to her career and her brother for so long that any other way of responding seemed abnormal.

But definitely easier for the time being, Brenna reflected a few hours later as she sat curled deep in the corner of the sofa in front of Ryder's fireplace. Much easier. She had spent the day sidestepping her problems, and the technique had some definite attractions. She smiled a little ruefully to herself as she sipped the excellent brandy and gazed into the flames.

The conversation all evening had been about philosophy and the characters in Ryder's books. Brenna had been drawn comfortably into the folds of the conversation, giving herself up to the safety of it with pleasure and undeniable relief. There had been no more talk of her career or of the claim Ryder was making, and over the past few hours she had finally relaxed.

At the opposite end of the sofa Ryder raised his brandy snifter in a small, intimate salute.

"To another perfect evening."

Brenna's lips curved as she turned her head to look at him. Her state of relaxation gave her the courage to tease now about a matter she would not have dared to bait him with a few hours earlier. "Perfect? Even though you'll be sleeping in your own bed tonight?"

As soon as she spoke the words Brenna regretted the impulse to tease. It was the first time the conversation had come back to sex all evening and she wished she hadn't been the one to bring it up now.

"My own bed," Ryder repeated thoughtfully. "There's nothing wrong with my bed. At least there are no stairs to climb." He hesitated long enough to catch her full attention. "Will I be sleeping alone in my bed, Brenna?"

Her head came up with a challenging movement. The room seemed suddenly very warm to Brenna. Keep it light, she told herself firmly. Keep it light.

"Don't worry, Ryder. You're safe enough tonight. I won't be seducing you."

"I've always had a certain reckless streak," he informed her gently. "Some forms of safety just don't appeal. I think you share the same brand of recklessness, Brenna Llewellyn." Very deliberately he sat up and placed his snifter on the brass-bound trunk in front of the sofa.

Brenna saw the waiting trap in the silver eyes and felt her pulse quicken. In fear or desire?

"You said you would wait," she reminded him, her voice a thread of sound.

"For an invitation," he agreed with a nod, making no move.

"There isn't going to be an invitation." But her fingers were trembling and she had to set down her snifter.

"No?" He put out a hand and traced a tiny design along the line of her throat. The erotic little caress made her catch her breath. The gold in Brenna's eyes was suddenly very warm. "Can you bring yourself to deny either of us tonight what we found last night?"

"Have you been seducing me with the philosophy and the brandy all night?" she tried to ask flippantly.

"No, you've been seducing me again," he whispered throatily. "Talking to you is a seduction in itself, lady. Don't you know that?"

With an effort of will Brenna got to her feet. "I think I'd better go, Ryder," she murmured. "Good night. Thank you for dinner." Wrenching her gaze away from his, she tried to snap the bonds settling around her. But every step toward the door was like a step through quicksand.

He was behind her, soft and silent and all leashed masculine power, when she put her hand on the doorknob.

"I have to go, Ryder." She stared down at her fingers as they tightened fiercely around the knob.

"I'm not stopping you."

"Damn it!" She looked up furiously. "You're not helping, either!"

"That would be asking too much, lady," he drawled very gently. "Far too much."

She wrenched open the door and came to a halt on the threshold, glaring out into the dark shadows. What did she want tonight? Surely she could not take the risk of letting this man make love to her again. Where was her common sense? Where was the rational, logical side of her nature when she needed it?

"Ryder, I can't stay tonight," she began tightly, whirling to face him. " But about last night. I want you to know...oh!"

When she swung around on the threshold, he was right behind her. She hadn't heard the step that brought him so close, but when she turned he was there and his arms came around her as she collided with the hard, compelling planes of his chest. Wordlessly she stood in the circle of his embrace, eyes very wide and questioning as she looked up into his taut features. She saw the hungry longing in him and couldn't move.

"Last night," he said very gently, "was perfect. Tonight will be perfect, too."

He swung her off her feet and into his arms. Turning, he kicked the door closed behind them and carried Brenna back toward the warmth of the fire.

Seven

Ryder lowered himself to the sofa with Brenna across his thighs. For a long moment he simply cradled her close. She nestled her head against his shoulder, aware of his lips hovering near her hair. He wanted her. She could feel the power of the hunger in him and knew the surge of desire in herself. It was easy, far too easy, to simply suspend all thought and give herself up to the night and the man who held her.

"Well, lady?" he prodded with carefully controlled urgency. "Do I get my invitation?"

"I thought you were inviting yourself." She lifted her lashes and raised a fingertip to toy with the curl of tawny hair on his neck.

"You'll have to say the words. I don't want there to be any question in your mind."

"About who is seducing whom?" she mocked softly.

"Exactly."

She felt the tension within and sought for a way out. "Ryder, I don't want the responsibility tonight. All day long I have been avoiding decisions about the important things in my life, and I don't want to make any decisions tonight. Do you understand?"

"I understand," he surprised her by saying. "You want me to make this particular decision. You want me to assume the responsibility for both of us."

She flinched. "That makes me very weak, doesn't it?"

"It makes you very vulnerable." He smiled crookedly, threading a hand through the dark chocolate of her hair and loosening the strands. "Are you sure you're ready to trust me to make the right choice? You must know I'm already convinced we belong together tonight."

"Don't talk to me about it," she cried softly. "I don't want to think about all the rational implications!"

"All right, sweet lady," he crooned, feathering her ear with his tongue. "Just remember in the morning that you turned all the responsibility over to me tonight."

Brenna didn't say anything; she couldn't. She relaxed against him with a small sigh of desire as the caress on her ear became damp and warm and teasing. Yes, it was much easier this way. She luxuriated in the sensation of being safe and warm and wanted.

Abandoning herself to the enthralling illusion being spun around her, Brenna moved her palm lovingly down Ryder's cheek to his throat. There she found the first of the buttons on his shirt and set about unfastening them. His breath fanned her ear and his hand slid up from her waist to seek out the shape of her breast.

"Ryder," she said on a long sigh as his thumb and forefinger coaxed forth the tight bud of her nipple beneath the fabric of her shirt. "Oh, Ryder..."

"You feel so right, so good in my hands," he whispered huskily as he undid the buttons of her shirt and moved his hand inside to cup the breast he had been teasing. "Thank you, sweet lady, for turning the decisions over to me tonight. You won't regret it."

Brenna, who didn't understand exactly what he was talking about, ignored the words and moved her lips tenderly to his throat as he traced patterns of desire across her breasts. She stirred as the delicious sensual tension began to build inside her and gloried in the evidence of his own rising passion.

When her fingers fluttered lightly down his chest, twining and untwining in the crisp, curling hair, he groaned urgently at the touch. The sound, uttered deep in his throat, emboldened her. She let her delicate fingertips wander lower until they settled lightly on the blatant male hardness covered by the fabric of his jeans.

"You see what you do to me?" he complained ruefully. "It's not easy for a man to be subtle when he wants a woman as badly as I want you!"

Brenna thrilled to the confession, experiencing a feminine power that was reflected in her amber eyes. Ryder saw it at once and laughed a little as he gathered her closer. "Witch," he growled. "Just remember you've turned all the authority over to me this evening!''

She smiled invitingly and lifted her mouth for his kiss. He obliged at once, his tongue surging hungrily between her lips. Slowly he lowered her down onto the cushions of the sofa, pressing her deep with his weight until she was thoroughly trapped. Her arms encircled his neck as he pushed aside her shirt and crushed her breasts against his chest.

Ryder built the fires in her with an insistent, persuasive rhythm that made it seem the most natural thing in the world for Brenna to surrender. She arched her hips upward into his as he lifted himself momentarily to slip off her shirt and his own.

Instead of coming back down on top of her at once, he boldly put his palm flat against the feminine mound still hidden by her jeans. His eyes met her heavy-lidded gaze as he waited for a moment, feeling her warmth. The touch was possessive to an incredible degree and the look in his eyes challenged her to acknowledge that possession.

''Tell me you want me, lady,'' he commanded with utmost gentleness.

''I want you, Ryder.'' The words were forced out from between dry lips and she automatically put the tip of her tongue to those lips after she had spoken.

''You take away my breath, lady.''

Slowly he undressed her under the flickering warmth of the firelight, and when she lay naked and bathed in gold before his gaze, he stood up long enough to tug off the black jeans he wore. Then he knelt beside the couch and ran his fingers from her throat to her ankles as she lay open to his touch.

Brenna's heated eyes wandered hungrily over the hard, sleek shape of him as he knelt beside her in the firelight. His tawny hair caught the flames, and the muscled contours of his shoulders drew her fingers. When she turned toward him convulsively, Ryder's hand on her thigh moved up along the delicate inside skin and probed the dark mystery between her legs.

"Oh!" The bold touch brought a gasping cry to her lips and she squeezed her lashes closed in response. Ryder leaned closer to kiss the tips of her aching breasts and she clutched at him, a tremor singing through her.

"Come here, sweet lady. I want to feel you all over me," he groaned and pulled her down on top of him as he lay back against the rug. Brenna sprawled across him in a tangle of silky skin and unbound hair.

Feeling marvelously pagan and excitingly wild, she began to do as he bid, scattering tiny, nipping kisses across his shoulders and down the hardness of his thighs. She reveled in his response, taking a primitive delight in seeing how far she could excite him before he lost his control. It was a game she had never played before and the danger implicit in it only acted as a lure.

He caught her head, his fingers winding tightly in her hair, and held her still for a moment so that he could drink from her lips. Then he released her once more and let her continue showering the tasting, impulse-driven kisses across his body.

When she rose briefly on her knees beside him, bending low to find the flat, masculine nipples with her mouth, he lifted his hand to trace the line of her spine down to the sensitive base. When she arched instinctively at the caress, he trailed his fingers further, sliding them erotically down her buttocks to the dampening warmth below.

''Oh, my God, Ryder,'' Brenna breathed, collapsing against him in an agony of passionate need. Her kisses became a little desperate as she reached out for him.

''Come and take me, sweet lady. Come and take me.''

Catching her hips, he guided her astride him, fitting her body to his with urgency. Brenna gasped at the uncompromising invasion of the throbbing heart of her passion. His fingers clenched deeply into her buttocks as he held her tightly and began to thrust upward with a surging power. She buried her lips in the curve of his shoulder and gave herself up to the wonder of the moment.

The sensual pace quickened and intensified until Brenna was moaning helplessly over and over again. Her nails raked unconsciously along the strong shoulders beneath her, and when she gave in to the impulse to sink her teeth lightly into his flesh, Ryder grunted.

Then, quite abruptly, she was on her back, the intimate connection of their bodies never broken in the process. With a muttered exclamation of need, Ryder surged against her, wrapping her to him until she felt utterly consumed. It became impossible to tell where the heat of her desire stopped and the heat of Ryder's body began.

As the passion flared higher between them Brenna could only cling and cling and go on clinging to the one rock-hard reality in her private universe. Ryder seemed to lose himself in her even as he demanded everything from her, and when the shattering culmination took them both, their husky cries of satisfaction mingled together.

In the aftermath of their sensual battle Brenna lay curled into Ryder's body, his hair-roughened thigh trapping her smooth one, his palm moving lazily along the curve of her hip. When he spoke, his mouth was close to her tangled hair.

"You're so incredibly responsive," he murmured wonderingly. "You seem to go up in flames in my arms. It's enough to make me want to keep you under lock and key. I couldn't bear to have another man so much as touch you now that you're mind, lady. I've never felt so...so..."

"Possessive?" Brenna supplied with a smile as she pulled back a little to look at him. "Chauvinistic? Demanding? Irrationally jealous?"

"You take the words right out of my mouth," he drawled on a note of dangerous humor as he dropped a kiss on the tip of her nose. "Take heed, lady, I shall be a very possessive, chauvinistic, demanding, and jealous lover."

"Your basic technique must be pretty good in spite of all those drawbacks," she retorted saucily, adding in a little rush as his silver eyes narrowed, "Because I've certainly never known what it feels like to go up in flames before."

"Brenna!"

He pulled her close, stroking the smooth contour of her back down to her waist. It was a moment of great tenderness, not passion, and Brenna found it captivating. She nestled against him, delighting in him. Together they lay watching the flickering flames on the hearth die.

A long time later Ryder got to his feet and led Brenna down the hall to his bedroom

"I should have just kept you here that first night when you climbed through my window," he said as he tucked her in beside him and found the tip of her breast with his fingers. "Much simpler."

But the next morning Brenna awoke with the feeling that things weren't going to be simple at all. She lay for a moment beside Ryder thinking of all the realities she had postponed facing the day before and wondered where to start. Slowly she turned her head to look at him, taking a subtle pleasure in the harshly carved planes of his face and the sprawled grace of his body.

He had seduced her yesterday, she thought wonderingly. But it was a seduction she would never be able to hold against him, for in his arms she had found a depth of feeling she wouldn't have guessed existed. With all her heart she was glad she had given him the invitation he had wanted last night.

But now morning had arrived and with it a return to the problems that needed solutions.

The tawny lashes shifted on the high ridge of his cheek as Ryder came awake and opened his eyes to meet her gaze. Without a word he put out a hand and dragged her face lazily down to his for a lingering kiss.

"Lady, you look very good here in my bed."

Dear God, Brenna thought as everything began to click into place at the sight of his contented, indulgent grin. I'm falling in love with the man. And it's all wrong. He's not the right one at all. He can't be!

"You wouldn't look so bad, yourself, if you could wipe that expression of smug, male satisfaction off your face," she tried to say lightly as she pulled free of him to sit up on the edge of the bed.

"Can you blame me for appearing a little relieved this morning now that I know I won't have to beg for invitations to your bed in the future?" He reached behind him and adjusted the pillows so that he could sit up against them. The silver eyes watched her with possessive pleasure as Brenna, clutching the sheet to her throat, turned to look at him.

Why did it have to be this man? Why couldn't it have been someone like Damon? Someone from her own world? Ryder Sterne was so different from everything she had known all her life…

"A gentleman always waits for an invitation, Ryder," she told him deliberately.

"Not after the lady has turned over the responsibility to him," he corrected with a knowing chuckle. "Last night you did exactly that, Brenna Llewellyn."

"For one night!"

"Forever."

She blinked, taken aback by the conviction in his tone. Try to keep it light, Brenna. She repeated the instructions over and over to herself. You must keep things light. There must be ways of handling this kind of an affair. Heaven help her! She needed time to think. She had to sort out the alarming mixture of her emotions for this man. Perhaps once she was free of the devastating intimacy of his bedroom, she would be able to think properly.

"Aren't you presuming a great deal on the basis of what happened last night?" she tried to say repressively.

"And the night before," he added helpfully. "Don't forget what happened the night before, either. Yes, I guess you could say I'm presuming." He reached out and snagged her wrist, yanking her down on top of him in a soft tumble. A silver devil laughed at her from the depths of his eyes, but there was tender possession in the touch of his hands as he smoothed her nakedness. "I'm presuming that I'm going to be the only man in your life, sweet lady. I'm presuming that you have given yourself to me and I'm presuming that you can't take back the rights you handed over last night when you turned over the responsibility for what happened to me."

"That's a hell of a lot of presumption!" she pointed out carefully as he cradled her forcefully in the crook of his arm.

"What are you going to do about it?" he provoked, refusing to appear the least concerned by her mood. "Allow me to point out that I'm bigger than you are."

He was only teasing her, Brenna told herself firmly, taking a short rein on her temper. She might be nervous and on edge because of the implications of the last two nights, but there was no need to lose her self-control just because he was in a playful mood. The intelligent way of handling this was to respond in kind. She must be cool and at ease with the situation until she could escape to think it over properly.

"Size is not always an asset," she noted demurely. "It didn't do the dinosaurs much good."

"A poor analogy. The dinosaurs didn't combine brain with brawn the way I do," he declared immodestly. He swept back the sheet, sliding his legs over the edge of the bed and getting to his feet. He stood grinning down at her, his hands on his lean hips for a moment. "Guess which of us is going to win in a one-on-one confrontation. All your fine philosophy isn't going to do you a bit of good in a situation like this!"

Before she could divine his intention, Ryder was reaching down to scoop her up and toss her lightly over his broad shoulder.

"Ryder! What the devil do you think you're doing? Put me down!" But she was laughing in spite of herself. The mood of boyish bravado and playfulness in him was difficult to withstand this morning. And she was falling in love with the man.

"I'm going to teach you how to scrub my back," he announced, spinning around to stride toward the bathroom. "I've always wanted my own personal back scrubber."

"A private fantasy of yours?" she demanded caustically. Deliberately she dug her nails into his side.

"Ouch!" he yelped and promptly retaliated by slapping her vulnerable, bare rear. "Damn right it's a private fantasy. Very private." He walked into the bath and turned on the shower, stepping into the stall itself with Brenna still draped over his shoulder.

"This is ridiculous," she groaned.

"Start scrubbing."

It was an hour before Brenna was finally able to free herself of the exuberant mood Ryder was indulging, and then it was only because she demanded an opportunity to go back to her cabin to put on some fresh clothes.

"If you'll settle down and promise to stop picking me up and bouncing me around as if I were a toy, I might even make you some breakfast," she volunteered before she could stop herself. The thought of making his breakfast was strangely pleasing. And he certainly had fed her enough lately.

"It's a deal," he agreed, sending her on her way with an affectionate pat on her derriere. With a last, wary glance over her shoulder, Brenna escaped.

But being alone for a while with her own thoughts did not prove to be the steadying, rational time Brenna had assumed it would be. She padded barefoot around her kitchen making pancakes from scratch and heating syrup and tried to think through the crisis in her life.

It wasn't fair that everything traumatic should be happening to her at once: her career at a crucial point; her love life dominated by someone who was not at all as she had secretly imagined the man of her dreams would be. It was just too much!

What was she going to do? She added the buttermilk to the pancake batter and told herself that as far as her career was concerned, she had to decide on a logical course of action that would also satisfy her own inner sense of honor and integrity. In some ways that crisis was going to be the easier one to deal with. But what did one do about falling in love with a man like Ryder Sterne? A man who, in his own words, found love a sloppy and sentimental emotion. A summer affair? She bit her lip in a rush of pain. It was difficult to think in such terms when one hovered on the brink of love…

She threw a chunk of butter on to the heating griddle as a knock came on the front door. It struck her as funny that Ryder should still be politely knocking after what they had shared during the past two days and she was smiling when she opened the door.

"Craig!"

Brenna took one startled look at the dark-haired young man on her doorstep and then hurled herself delightedly into his arms. "Craig Llewellyn, did you come all the way up here to see me or are you here to mooch a few free days at Tahoe!" Laughing, she hugged her brother and stepped back. "You're just in time for breakfast. Come on in."

"Thanks, you know I'm always available for a free meal. How's it going up here, Brenna? Having a good summer?" Craig stepped into the room, his arm draped around his sister's shoulders. He had inherited the deep brown hair of all the Llewellyns and the gold in his amber eyes matched Brenna's, but she had always privately thought him rather handsome into the bargain. The natural bias of a sister, she decided warmly, glancing up at him. His body had a young man's lean ranginess, which reflected his interest in outdoor pursuits. The planes of his face were maturing into strong features. She already knew he didn't lack for female companionship although he'd never gotten overly serious about anyone since the night of his high school prom when he'd come home convinced he was in love. The emotion, however, had faded within a week, Brenna remembered. She had been enormously thankful at the time.

"Is everything okay back in Berkeley? In thought you were taking some summer classes this year?"

"Everything's fine," Craig said slowly, taking a seat at the table while she puttered around the kitchen.

Brenna looked up at the careful steadiness in his words. "I'm glad to see you, Craig, but how is it you're here during the week? I would have thought you wouldn't have any free time until the weekend. I know how intensive summer classes usually are."

He seemed to take a long breath. "Brenna, I came up here to talk to you about…about next year."

She froze, straightening from the drawer where she had been looking for an extra setting of stainless. "Next year?"

"Brenna, I'm not going back to school in the fall."

All the other crises in Brenna's life were quickly pushed to a back burner. "Oh, Craig, no! You're not going to drop out! Not now when you're so close to finishing. You can't!"

The breakfast preparations forgotten, she came across the room in a daze to stand at the opposite side of the table. Her face was a mask of anxiety and protest. Two pairs of amber eyes stared at each other in pain and determination.

"Brenna, please try to understand. I've had enough of school. I want…I want to go out and see a little of the world. I have an opportunity to get a job on a freighter next month."

"A freighter!"

The young man's mouth tightened at the disbelief in her voice, but he kept his own tone level and desperately reasonable. "It's a unique opportunity and it's something I want to do very badly. It feels right for me, Brenna, do you know what I mean? This past year at the university hasn't had the feeling of being right. I've just been marking time..."

"Well, can't you mark another year of it? Craig, your education is so important, you must see that! You can't abandon it all now!" Her fingers curled into the wood as she clutched the chair in front of her. "It's only another year."

"And then I'll have a degree for which I have no use. Brenna, I'm a history major, for God's sake. Do you realize what that means? The only thing I can do with that is go on to graduate school and that's the last thing I want!"

"It makes a hell of a lot more sense than shipping out on some damn freighter! Craig, that's like a kid talking of running off to join the circus! It's crazy!"

"It's what I want," he repeated quietly. Craig's hand was coiled as tightly as Brenna's. She read the determination in him and wanted to cry with frustration. To have come so far and then give it all up now. It was wrong. Very wrong. She had to convince him.

"Please, Craig," she tried, keeping her voice under control with a tremendous effort. "There's only one more year to go. After that you can decide if you really want to leave the academic life altogether. But at least you'll have that degree to fall back on if you ever change your mind."

''I can always go back to school to finish if that's what I want to do...''

For the second morning in a row Brenna was so wrapped up in the tension generated by an early visitor that she failed to hear the front door of the cabin open. The first either she or Craig knew of Ryder's presence was the sound of his dangerously laconic voice behind her brother.

''This is getting to be a habit, isn't it? Finding strange men sitting down to have breakfast with you in the mornings is not one of my favorite ways to start a day.''

''Ryder!'' Brenna looked up quickly, her eyes suddenly anxious for reasons other than the immediate crisis with Craig. ''Wait, this is...''

But Craig was already getting to his feet to face the newcomer. He was apparently unruffled by the challenge in the older man's words. There was a physical tension in him that Brenna read at once as preparation for battle, but when he spoke, Craig's voice was calm and clear.

''I'm Craig Llewellyn.'' He waited as Ryder assessed him with a cool silver glance. ''Brenna is my sister.''

''Yes, with those eyes and that hair, you'd have to be related, wouldn't you?'' The moment of strain dissolved as Ryder stuck out his hand, his grin inviting Craig to forgive the brief male challenge that had threatened for a few seconds. ''I'm Ryder Sterne.''

Craig accepted the proffered hand and accompanied the handshake with a searching, curious smile.

"You obviously feel you have some right to be concerned with other men at Brenna's breakfast table?"

"Craig Llewellyn!" Brenna gasped, horrified.

"Every right in the world," Ryder was saying easily, sinking lithely into one of the chairs and smiling with brilliant casualness at an infuriated Brenna. "She belongs to me, you see."

"Don't listen to him, Craig," Brenna instructed tightly as her brother reacted with only a mildly inquiring eyebrow. "He's been in this...this *teasing* mood all morning."

"All morning?" Craig glanced speculatively from Ryder to his sister, the question-behind-the-question there for all to hear.

Brenna, for the first time in her life, felt as if the tables had been somehow turned between her brother and herself. Suddenly it was her little brother who was questioning her actions. She knew the flush in her cheeks was not going to go unnoticed by either man at the breakfast table. Hurriedly Brenna got to her feet.

"Would either of you care for a cup of tea?" she demanded frostily.

"She's still a little shy about the situation," Ryder explained to Craig.

"Understandable." Craig nodded, still eyeing his table mate. "The kind of men Brenna usually dates don't generally go around claiming she belongs to them. They tend to talk a slightly different line."

"In asked if either of you wanted any tea!"

"That will be fine, Brenna," Ryder agreed soothingly. "I'm sure Craig will have some, too." As she turned to put on the teakettle he asked Craig interestedly, ''What kind of line do they usually talk?''

''You have to understand that there haven't been all that many men in her life,'' Craig answered reflectively.

''During the years I was in high school, she had her hands full making a home for me and getting her career started. It didn't leave her much time for a social life. Lately the one or two men she's introduced me to have been the kind who talked about career-oriented partnerships and having intellectual interests in common. They tended to worry a great deal about personal freedom in a relationship and not being stifled by such outmoded concepts as possessiveness. The kind of guys who would probably be involved in affairs with their graduate students six months after marrying Brenna.''

''Craig!'' White-faced, Brenna whirled to confront her brother. ''You've said enough. Please shut up!''

''I'm sorry, Brenna,'' he apologized at once, sensing her genuine anger and embarrassment. ''You're already upset. I shouldn't have teased you like that,'' he sighed ruefully.

''Why are you already upset?'' Ryder demanded as she began to pour pancake batter with an unsteady hand.

''It's a private matter between Craig and myself,'' she told him stiffly.

''If you're this upset about it, you'd better tell me what's going on,'' he returned coolly. She could feel his narrowed, searching gaze on her taut profile but she refused to look at him.

''I don't wish to talk about it,'' she stated flatly.

Ryder pinned Craig matter-of-factly. "Are you in trouble?"

Craig straightened a little warily at the chilled softness in the older man's voice. "No," he said quickly. "No, I'm not in trouble. I'm…I'm dropping out of school. That's what I came to tell Brenna."

"And that's why she's upset? What are you going to do, Craig?"

Brenna set down the pitcher of pancake batter and stared in frozen silence as the two men faced each other. She had obviously been cut out of the conversation completely. Or perhaps she'd cut herself out when she'd refused to discuss the matter with Ryder.

Craig hesitated and then plunged earnestly into the reasons behind his decision. In a few minutes he had summed it up, and when he sat back in his chair, Brenna had the impression he was awaiting Ryder's opinion as if it really mattered.

Ryder was silent for a while. He folded his elbows on the table and fixed a considering glance on Craig's expectant features. "You're absolutely certain this is what you want to do?"

"Absolutely certain," Craig vowed feelingly. He didn't look at Brenna, who stood taut and silent by the stove.

"What's the name of the freighter line?"

Craig told him and Ryder nodded thoughtfully. "I've heard of it. They've been around a while. Do you know anything about working on a freighter?"

"Not much," Craig admitted. "They said I'd be trained."

Ryder's mouth tilted upward sardonically. "I'm sure you will be. It's hard work, Craig."

"I know."

"Have you ever been to sea at all?"

"No, not really."

"Well," Ryder suddenly announced calmly, "I'm sure you'll find it very interesting. Remember you can always jump ship if the going gets too rough. It's not like signing on with the military."

Craig's relief at Ryder's apparent approval was blatantly obvious. "I'll keep that in mind. Have you ever done anything like it yourself?"

Ryder paused and then said quietly, "I've done a little traveling the hard way. Seeing how the rest of the world functions is a very educational experience. Probably be worth five or ten years in graduate school!"

"That's enough! Both of you!" Brenna's fury boiled over as they shifted their glances to her tense face. "Craig, this is absolute nonsense and you know it. Ryder, you have no right to encourage him like that! This is a family matter between Craig and myself and I demand that you stay out of it!"

"Lady, you know anything that concerns you, concerns me. This is a decision Craig has to make for himself. He's a man in addition to being your little brother. He has to make up his own mind about what he wants to do with his life."

"You don't understand!" she wailed, feeling at her wits' end. "He's only got one more year of school! He's come this far, why can't he finish? Ryder, what if something happens? What if he gets into trouble like the Gardners' son did?"

Ryder looked at her. "If he gets into trouble I'll go and get him out of it," he stated with gentle simplicity.

Brenna stared at him helplessly for an instant longer as a wave of panic and defeat rolled over her. Then, without a word, she turned and walked out of the cabin, leaving the pancakes to burn on the griddle.

Eight

No one pursued Brenna to try to soothe her or "talk sense into her," and for that she was inordinately grateful. She needed time to think and to adjust. Her sense of responsibility toward her younger brother had existed for so many years, she realized, that it had become almost maternal in nature.

Her mouth twisted ruefully even as the tears stung her eyes. She stood, hands jammed into the front pockets of her jeans, and stared out at the calm surface of the lake. She had walked far enough to be out of sight of the cabins.

Craig was a man now, she told herself. A young man who lacked experience, it was true, but still a man. Ryder had been right to correct her when she had termed her brother a "kid" a few days ago. Even mothers had to let go when the time came, Brenna reminded herself. It was still more important that she, who was not his mother, step out of the responsibility role. After all, she wanted herself and Craig to be friends. It would be unhealthy and stupid to try to persist in the dominant older sister mode.

Funny, she'd never thought of herself as domineering, but when she'd heard herself yelling at her younger brother that he had to stay in college, there was no denying the fact that she had assumed too much responsibility, for too long.

Not that Craig was going to allow her to control his life, apparently, she added wryly. He had come up to Lake Tahoe to break the news to her, not to ask her advice in the matter.

She thought of the tale of the Gardners' son, the one Ryder had been hired to rescue from a foreign prison, and shuddered. Working on a freighter, Craig was bound to encounter the rougher side of life. What if he wound up in real trouble? Her imagination worked overtime supplying possibilities.

Brenna put a halt to that line of thought with a firm mental decision. Craig was not Evan Gardner. He was not a mixed-up kid engaging in an act of rebellion. He was simply ready to start living his own life. And if he got in trouble Ryder would go and get him and bring him home.

Ryder. He had promised her that much and she could trust him. Brenna turned from the shore and started back toward the cabins.

The two men had apparently finished breakfast on their own, Brenna realized as she walked back into her cabin. The dishes had been piled in the sink and the griddle turned off. She was warming it back up again in preparation for her own meal when she glanced out the window and saw Ryder and Craig in front of the archery target.

For a few minutes she simply watched, ignoring the sizzling griddle as Ryder demonstrated shooting techniques to the younger man. Craig appeared fascinated and picked up the basics quickly. Even as she stared at the two men, Brenna slowly acknowledged that Craig and Ryder had a lot in common. There was a self-reliant masculine assurance and determination in both of them that would always set its own standards. They were the kind of men who lived by their own codes and for whom honor and integrity would always be crucial. The kind of men a woman could trust to the ends of the earth even when she became thoroughly annoyed or outraged by the host of macho characteristics that went along with their honor and integrity. Brenna turned away from the window and sat down to eat her pancakes.

It was Craig who came back to the cabin an hour or so later, alone. He looked concerned but very determined. Brenna glanced up from the essay on the dualism of mind and matter that she was attempting to read and smiled. The expression was a bit misty, perhaps even wistful, but it was a genuine smile and Craig relaxed visibly. His mouth lifted in response, and for a moment brother and sister stared at each other in understanding. Then Craig came forward and slipped into the chair across from Brenna.

"It's going to be okay, Brenna, Ryder's going to look after you for me," he said gently.

Brenna, who hadn't been thinking along those lines at all, blinked in astonishment. "What on earth are you talking about, Craig?"

He shrugged, sensing her sudden wariness. "Ryder and I had a long talk and he let me know how things stand between the two of you. He's going to take care of you. I won't have to worry about your marrying some turkey like that Fielding character."

Some of the wistful, sisterly gentleness faded from Brenna's startled eyes. "Craig, I don't know exactly what Ryder told you about our relationship, but I can assure you it is only temporary at best. Furthermore, it's not important at the moment. You're the one who is embarking on a new adventure and I...I want you to know that if this is what you really want to do, I'm behind you a hundred percent."

He leaned forward and hugged her affectionately. "Thanks, Brenna. I know what it must have taken for you to come to that conclusion. I know how important the academic world has been to you, and it was only natural you'd feel more comfortable putting me in that world, too. But it's not for me."

"I think I've sensed that for the past couple of years. The problem has been that it was the only world I knew, the only one I could guide you toward," she sighed.

"A man has to find out for himself where he belongs," Craig announced very solemnly. "It's time I went out and started looking."

They spent the rest of the day together, talking quietly, sharing the closeness of being a brother and sister who had been alone together in the world for a long time. Ryder discreetly disappeared into his own cabin and didn't reappear until Craig went over to invite him for dinner.

Brenna glanced up from the stuffed mushrooms she was removing from the oven and met his calm, inquiring gaze as he walked in the door behind Craig. Wordlessly he was asking her if she had accepted her brother's decision.

The answer to that one, she found, was easy. "Hello, Ryder. Have a seat. Craig has picked up a few interesting skills this past year. He mixes a terrific margarita. If he got that much out of Berkeley, there's no telling what he'll pick up on a freighter in the South Seas!" She laughed, sliding the hot pan of mushrooms quickly onto the top of the stove.

"A margarita sounds great, Craig." Ryder settled into one of the chairs in front of the hearth as Brenna carried in the plate of stuffed mushrooms. Craig headed for the kitchen with a grin and Brenna was left to face the second question in Ryder's eyes alone. The answer to that one, however, was not so easy. He must have known that Craig had told his sister of Ryder's decision to "take care of her." The silver gaze was asking her point-blank if she had accepted that decision, too.

"You have, I understand, been attempting to reassure my brother that I'll be all right in his absence," she began dryly, taking the bull by the horns as she sat down across from him.

"He was worried about you," Ryder said simply, reaching for one of the hors d'oeuvres. If he sensed the challenge in her words, he chose to ignore it. He bit into the mushroom. "These are great. Do you realize this is the first meal you've finally gotten around to preparing for me?"

"Ryder, Craig seems to have a slight misconception about our relationship," Brenna pursued firmly.

"No, he doesn't." Ryder was glancing past her shoulder to where Craig was coming toward them with a pitcher of margaritas and three salt-rimmed glasses. He grinned appreciatively at the younger man. "I'm glad to see there are still benefits to be derived from a university education."

After that there really was no opportunity to confront Ryder again. Craig was leaving to return to Berkeley in the morning, and Brenna was suddenly anxious not to cause a scene. Somehow it had become very important that the three of them enjoy this evening together. The other crises in her life could wait.

She let Craig and Ryder do most of the talking that evening, listening quietly as they discussed Craig's new venture and Ryder told a few anecdotes about some of his own travels. Ryder did not, Brenna noticed, bring up any incidents such as the assault on the prison that had freed the Gardners' son. For that she was grateful. Craig's future promised to be adventuresome enough without actively encouraging him into any more dangerous directions.

It wasn't until Ryder finally rose to walk back to his own cabin that Brenna finally acknowledged the evening had aroused a new kind of wistfulness in her. The talk had been of adventure and travel and personal discovery. It left her with a strange feeling of restlessness.

Ryder kissed her good night before he left, making no effort to conceal the extent of their relationship in front of Craig. She was the one who pulled back in confusion and embarrassment. But Craig only smiled, appearing satisfied with the situation as he chose to interpret it.

In spite of all her fine resolutions and understanding, there were tears in Brenna's eyes the next morning as she stood with Ryder's arm around her waist, waving goodbye to Craig, who was backing his car out of the drive.

"It's not as if he's going off to war," Ryder teased sardonically as Craig's car disappeared from sight. "And you'll be seeing him again before he ships out on the freighter, anyway."

"I know." Brenna dashed the dampness away from her eyes with a fierce brush of her hand. She stepped out of the circle of Ryder's arm.

"He'll be all right, Brenna. He's not an immature boy, he's a man."

"I know." Brenna started back toward her cabin, not looking at Ryder. The strange restlessness was eating at her. Her emotions seemed to be confusingly scrambled this morning. The traumatic events of the past week were taking their toll. She was aware that Ryder was pacing along beside her, frowning.

"Are you angry at me for sanctioning his decision to go?" he finally demanded softly.

Brenna said nothing. She wasn't sure how she felt just then. She couldn't define her emotions toward Ryder at that moment.

"He would have gone anyway, you know. There was no one who could have stopped him." She sensed Ryder's laconic smile. "He's got his sister's will and determination, I'm afraid."

Brenna bit her lip and still said nothing. She was filled now with a tension that threatened to force an outlet for itself. It angered her because she could not deal with the emotion until she understood it, and it seemed totally incomprehensible.

"Are you upset because I told Craig not to worry about you? That I would take care of you?"

Brenna shrugged, unable to speak. She needed time to herself, she thought. Time to come to terms with this strange, uncoiling tension. She started to push open the door to her cabin and behind her Ryder finally lost his patience.

"Damn it, Brenna! Talk to me! Don't just walk away from this!"

"What the hell do you think you're doing?" she gasped furiously as he clamped a large hand on her shoulder and whirled her around to face him.

"I'm trying to figure out what's gotten into you. I thought you'd come to grips with Craig's decision to leave!" He clamped the other hand on her shoulder and held her in front of him with a grip of iron. The brackets at the edges of his mouth were tight with impatience and the silver eyes were narrowed with it.

"I have come to grips with it!" she flung back, the tension in her crashing toward the surface. "No, I'm not upset with you for sanctioning his decision, either. What else could I have expected from you? You're two of a kind, you and Craig. It was perfectly natural that you'd understand him immediately!"

"Then you must be angry about the way I told him not to worry about you!" He punctuated his words by giving her a small shake.

"Maybe," she hissed, trying unsuccessfully to free herself from his hold. "Maybe I am a little upset about the way you handled that! You certainly didn't have any right to imply the sort of relationship you did!"

"The hell I didn't," he ground out far too gently. "Brenna, you're my woman now and I'll take care of you. It's as simple as that."

"Nothing is as simple as that!" she blazed, the gold of her eyes flaming as she faced him.

"Is that issue the real problem this morning?" He searched her face coolly. "You want a knockdown, drag-out fight over the matter of my claim on you?"

"No, damn it! I don't want a battle over it. That would be admitting your 'claim' exists in the first place!"

"It does."

"It can't exist unless I accept it!" she stormed. "But believe it or not, that's not the reason I'm upset this morning!"

"So tell me the reason," he ordered softly, implacably.

"It's none of your business!"

"Don't be ridiculous," he drawled quietly. "Of course it's my business. Everything about you is my business. Talk, woman. What's driving you this morning? Why are you tense and nervous and spoiling for a fight?"

"You don't think I've had enough cause for an emotional outburst of some magnitude?" she snapped furiously. "It's been a rough summer so far and my vacation's hardly begun!"

"You've had cause, but you were handling things fairly well. What happened this morning?"

"I don't know," she almost wailed. "It's too hard to explain and I really don't want to talk about it. Not with anyone!"

"You're going to talk about it with me."

"This may be a little tough for you to comprehend, Ryder Sterne, but you do not have the right to dictate to me like that!"

"Brenna, so help me, if you don't stop raving and tell me what the hell is wrong, I'm going to lose my temper," he stated flatly.

"Is that supposed to throw me into abject terror?"

"It might," he murmured. It struck her that the louder she got the quieter he was getting. It was alarming.

"That's a poor threat, Ryder. We all know you don't lose your temper. You're cool and calm and *professional* under fire, remember?"

"You really are looking for some method of venting your frustration, aren't you? You're even trying to provoke me so you'll have some reason to lash back. That's a dangerous game, lady. Much safer just to talk out the situation, believe me."

"I thought you favored the use of violence as a means of settling problems!"

"Only under certain circumstances," he drawled. "I don't think this is one of those circumstances. Yet. Now talk, Brenna."

"I can't even explain it to myself, let alone someone else," she whispered tersely. "Let me go, Ryder. I need to think."

There was a pause but he didn't release her. For

a few seconds he stared down into her simmering gaze and then he asked very coolly. "Are you by any chance jealous?"

"Jealous! *Jealous!*" she ripped out, stunned. "Of what, for God's sake! Are you hiding a model from one of your book covers somewhere nearby? Don't be absurd, Ryder! Of course I'm not jealous."

"Not of another woman. Of Craig."

The simple explanation hit home with an impact that took Brenna's breath. Her eyes went very wide with anguished denial and her body went rigid in his grasp. "Of Craig!" she repeated in a whisper.

"Of the fact that he's stepping out of the academic world and going off to indulge his natural streak of recklessness and taste for adventure. Do you see him having the courage to make the move and wish you had that courage, too?"

"No! No, that's not it at all! It can't be!"

"Why not? It makes sense to me, lady. There's no denying the intellectual side of your nature. Indeed, you've honed that aspect of yourself very nicely, given it every opportunity to express itself. But there's another side of you, isn't there, Brenna? A side you've always treated with disdain and kept repressed because you're afraid it will conflict with the lifestyle you admire most, the academic world."

Helplessly she looked up at him. It was the truth. She knew it and she didn't want to face it. Fear was the emotion that roiled within her now.

"That's why you're wary of me and my claim on you, isn't it?" he pursued steadily as he worked the implications through in his mind. "Giving yourself to me is a risk because I represent another kind of life, something far different from the one you've been trained to admire. Well, it's true, I'm not part of your college faculty world and I never will be, but you've already taken the risk, sweet lady. It's too late to change your mind. Find the courage to face our relationship the same way you found the courage to face Craig's decision and the way you'll find the courage to handle the crisis in your career!''

"Ryder, you don't know what you're saying!"

"Yes, I do. It's not a crisis in your career or with your brother's future that you're really facing this summer. You're having to make a very fundamental decision about what you want out of life."

"I know what I want out of life!"

"Yes," he surprised her by agreeing, "I think you do know what you want. The question is, are you going to have the guts to acknowledge that fact? How long will it take you to accept that for you there must be something more in life than the climb up the academic ladder and relationships with men like Damon Fielding who don't know what it means to want and need a woman the way I want and need you? Craig found the courage to strike out on his own and go after what he wants in life. How about you, Brenna? Will you find the same courage or will you scurry back to your ivory tower and force me to come drag you out of it?''

Appalled, Brenna tried to reason with herself. She must not let him do this to her! She was a rational, intelligent human being who knew how to think her way through any situation. She would not let this man drive her to violence. But she was trembling with a combination of outrage and fear as she bit out,

"If I decide to scurry home to my ivory tower, as you so graphically put it, I assure you there's no way on earth you'll be able to drag me back out! I make my own decisions in life and I will not let you control or manipulate me. Just because you've shared a bed with me on two occasions, don't get the idea you have any rights over me! How many times do I have to tell you that?"

"How many times do I have to take you to bed before you stop denying my rights?" he countered roughly.

It was too much. The events of the preceding days took their toll with a vengeance. And Ryder became the unlucky focus of all the chaotic emotions surging through her in that moment.

Brenna slapped him. Her hand moved in a wide, swinging arc that he probably could have avoided but didn't. Instead he just stood there and let her fingers create a bright-red brand on the side of his face.

The silence that followed seemed to extend even to the surrounding woods. In utter quiet Brenna stood staring at the man she had just struck, her mind numb with shock at her own behavior. Ryder didn't move.

"The thing about violence," he finally cautioned in a very gentle voice, "is that you have to be prepared for the possibility that it will escalate."

She swallowed. "Is that a way of saying you're going to get even?"

"Do you think I would really hit you?" He appeared almost curious.

Brenna closed her eyes in shame and self-disgust. "No. I deserve it but you won't do it." She took a couple of slow breaths, bringing herself back under control. When she opened her eyes, Ryder was already several feet away, walking back toward his cabin. She could only stand and watch as he moved off with that fog-silent step. He didn't look back.

It wasn't long after she'd served herself a lonely dinner in front of the fire and was focusing on the prospect of going to bed without even being able to say good night to Ryder that Brenna finally realized it was up to her to end the impasse. She was the one who had created it.

Ryder hadn't emerged from his cabin since he'd walked away after she'd lost her self-control. She could only presume that he'd spent the afternoon and evening beginning work on his book. He was probably the type who could do just that, she told herself unhappily. He was so damn self-controlled, he could probably put the incident with her out of his mind in disgust and go to work. She, on the other hand, couldn't get past page one of the quarterly issue of the philosophy journal in her lap.

Lifting her eyes from the open journal to the flames on the hearth, Brenna tried to rationalize her way out of what she knew, deep down, had to be done. Ryder had no real rights over her, she reminded herself, regardless of how he'd chosen to interpret her willingness to let him make love to her. It would probably be best to let the rift between them stand. It would serve to break off a relationship in which she was swiftly becoming far too involved. Only this morning she had found herself toying with the idea of falling in love with the man.

No, it would be simpler to use the current unpleasantness as a way of easing herself out of a highly precarious situation. It was frightening to think how close she had been to admitting she was in love with a man who was all wrong for her.

All wrong. It was crazy, ludicrous, and adolescent to allow one's emotions to rule one's head that far! Ryder was *different*, far different from any other man she had ever met. It stood to reason that there would be a certain attraction about him, didn't it? But that didn't mean a genuine, solid relationship could be built on that attraction. Sound relationships weren't built on the basis of a man declaring himself in possession of a woman because she had been foolish enough to surrender herself to him!

But even as she lectured herself, Brenna knew there was more to it than that. Unwillingly she recalled the hero of *The Quicksilver Venture*, a man hardened in the ways of the shadowy world in which he moved but still a man who lived by a code of honor and integrity; a man who could, in a strange way, be trusted. Not unlike Ryder.

No, Brenna told herself firmly, she had no business getting involved with a man like Ryder Sterne. The Damon Fieldings of this world were the kind of men she should be cultivating. Damon understood her lifestyle, her ambitions, and her career. He held modern views on the subject of a relationship, and just because Craig hadn't cared for the man, that didn't mean Damon was wrong for her. Heaven knew Craig was a lot more likely to view the world the way Ryder viewed it! They were two of a kind in many ways.

But Brenna Llewellyn was her own woman who had to make her own path and her own choices. It was all very well for Craig to choose a more adventuresome path in this world, but she, Brenna, had already chosen hers and it did not lead in the same direction. It did not lead toward men like Ryder Sterne.

None of which, she realized grimly, changed the fundamental question before her now. She owed Ryder an apology. Even if the wiser course of action might be to let the situation stand, there was still a matter of simple honor and simple manners involved.

She not only owed him an apology for the slap, she also owed him her thanks for the quiet way he had helped both her and Craig through the difficult time yesterday. His calm, reasonable attitude had been a source of reassurance for her, and clearly he'd had the same effect on her brother, who had been worrying about Brenna's reaction to his announcement.

Yes, she owed Ryder for that and for the slap. Her pride demanded that she take some step toward satisfying its demands. With a soft sigh Brenna got to her feet and located the rust-colored suede jacket she'd brought with her. It was going to be quite chilly outside this late at night.

As she stepped outside her door Brenna saw at once that there was no light on in the cabin across the clearing. Had Ryder gone to bed early? She glanced down at her watch. It was later than she had realized. Perhaps this whole thing should wait until morning.

But something drove her forward. This wasn't going to keep until morning. It had to be done as soon as possible. Too much time had already passed. As she walked across the clearing Brenna reminded herself over and over that going to Ryder like this involved nothing more than an apology and her personal thanks for what he had done for her and Craig. It most definitely did not involve any admission on her part that she was accepting the claim he had placed on her!

She bit her lip as she neared the cabin and realized that even the porch light was off. He must have gone to bed. Well, he would just have to get out of bed to hear what she had to say, she decided determinedly. Having made up her mind, Brenna knew she wasn't going to abandon the project now. With a firm step she began to circle around to the front door of the cabin. Then, quite suddenly, she realized she was about to pass by the open bedroom window. The window she had attempted to crawl through that first night.

Irresistibly Brenna was drawn to a halt beside the window. Ryder would be in there. All she had to do was rap on the panes and he would hear her. There would be darkness to cover her as she made her apology. She wouldn't have to stand in the full glare of the porch light and do it. The idea became incredibly appealing.

She moved a little closer to the open window and lifted a hand to tap on the glass. Nothing could be seen inside the shadow-filled room. Cautiously she scratched at the panes.

"Ryder?" she called very softly.

There was no answer; no sound from within. Brenna tapped gently once more. "Ryder, it's me,

Brenna. I have to talk to you. Just for a minute.''
Why the devil was she whispering?

When there was still no answer, she gnawed reflectively on her lower lip and thought seriously
about returning to her own cabin. In the morning she
could come back and do this in broad daylight.

That thought was enough to urge her into one
more effort. With every fiber of her being, Brenna
wanted to get the matter out of the way tonight. Deliberately she pushed the window open wider and
leaned inside the room. She still couldn't see much
except the vague outline of the end of the bed. In the
poor light she couldn't even tell if he was *in* the bed.
Brenna frowned and threw a leg over the sill.

''Ryder? Are you awake?''

She was sitting astride the windowsill now, peering into the gloom. Perhaps he was in the bathroom
brushing his teeth. Maybe he hadn't gone to bed yet
after all.

''I'm awake.''

The soft growl didn't come from the bed, it ema-
nated from directly behind her shoulder, from the
darkness inside the room at the edge of the window.
Brenna gasped and instinctively tried to slip her leg
off the sill so that she could stand safely outside the
window. He put a stop to that by putting out a hand
and clamping it strongly across her thigh. Automatically Brenna went very still as he moved into the
pale starlight coming in through the window. When
she found his face in the darkness, she drew in her
breath a little shakily. He looked very dangerous
there in the shadows. He was wearing only a pair of
Jockey shorts, and the lean, sinewy lines of his body

seemed quite pagan. The expression in his silvery eyes was totally unreadable but the hand on her thigh was easily comprehended. He wasn't going to let her slip back outside the window.

"Good lord!" she breathed. "You frightened me. I thought you'd be in bed. When you didn't answer my tap on the window, I decided you must not be in the room."

"I heard you crunching around outside on the gravel. I wasn't quite sure what to think about having you attempt to crawl through my window, though, so I thought I'd give it a few minutes to see how far you intended to go. Now you're here shall I draw my own conclusions?" The fingers on her thigh tightened but she still couldn't make out the emotion behind his silver gaze.

Brenna decided to plunge into her explanation without delay. That was the reason she had come to his cabin, wasn't it? "Ryder, I'm here for—for several reasons."

He waited, one brow arching slightly.

"First of all, I owe you an apology for what happened this morning after Craig left…" She forced herself to go on in a steady voice. "I lost my self-control. There was absolutely no excuse for that and I can only say I'm sorry. Violence is never an answer!"

"But it can, as I pointed out earlier, give one a feeling of satisfaction," he returned dryly.

"Well, it didn't," she muttered icily. "I'm ashamed of myself and it only served to make me feel like a fool. My only excuse is that I was on edge at the time."

"Yes." There was a pause, and when she didn't say anything else, he questioned carefully, "And your other reasons for climbing through my window tonight?"

Brenna stifled a groan. He wasn't going to make this easy. "I wanted to thank you for helping Craig and me. You somehow managed to reassure both of us and keep things calm. I think the situation would have been a great deal more unpleasant if you hadn't been there. It—it helped when you said that if Craig ever got himself into real trouble you'd go and get him out, and I know Craig felt better when you told him you'd look after me. Oh, I can't explain it exactly, Ryder. It was just that your presence made things easier for my brother and for me."

"I see. Anything else?"

Brenna hesitated. She hadn't meant to tell him the rest. There was no need to confess everything, especially this last matter about which she still wasn't very certain herself. But a rush of self-honesty, aided by the comforting blanket of darkness, brought the words to the surface. "You—you may have been right about my being a little envious of my brother," she mumbled.

"Because he made the break you didn't make years ago?" His tone was gently implacable. There was no sympathy in it at all.

"Perhaps a part of me wonders what would have happened if I hadn't chosen the path I did. But that's natural, isn't it? Everyone must think along those lines from time to time. I did choose the academic world, however, and it's been satisfying. It's my life now and I'm content with it. I'm not like you or Craig.''

''Not even a little bit like us?''

''No,'' she stated very firmly. ''No, and even if I were, it's too late. I made my choice a long time ago.''

''It's never too late, Brenna,'' he told her softly. ''There are no rules that say we have to stay committed to any single job or career. The only rules we have to follow in life are the ones we make for ourselves.''

''I'm happy in my world, damn it,'' she suddenly flared. ''I'm good at what I do and it's satisfying. I may wonder occasionally about the other side of life, the kind of life you have explored, but that doesn't mean I want to explore it for myself. I'm a teacher of philosophy and that's enough for me. I don't entertain any secret admiration for the more adventuresome life. Hell, I probably wouldn't even approve of many of the things you've done, much less admire them! I do admire my own world, or at least a great deal of it,'' she added, thinking of the aspect of it she had been exposed to lately when Paul Humphrey had stolen her work. But there were honorable and dishonorable people in every profession, weren't there?

''Okay,'' Ryder said soothingly, ''so you're happy in your ivory tower. That's your decision.''

''Thanks!''

''But that still leaves one more issue, Brenna.''

She looked at him with sudden wariness. ''What issue?''

''The matter of our relationship. I have a claim on

you, lady, and you can't rationalize or argue or philosophize your way out of that. I'm waiting for you to accept it intellectually just as you've accepted it with your body.''

''No!'' She made a startled movement, and his hand on her thigh clenched with gentle warning. ''Ryder, you and I are from two different worlds.''

''That's got nothing to do with it.''

''But it does! I need someone from the academic world. Someone who understands my career and my way of thinking. What you and I have together is a very temporary thing. You need someone who's more—more exciting and venturesome.''

''We want and need each other, lady,'' he interrupted quietly. ''How much longer until you realize that?''

''What about love?'' she flung back, aware that she was inserting a totally irrational argument into what should have stayed a very rational discussion.

''What about love?'' he countered. ''I'm talking about fundamentals, not vague, indefinable concepts like love. You're an intelligent woman: face the facts of the situation. You want me, even if you are a little afraid of me at this point.''

''I am not afraid of you!'' she bit out furiously.

''Yes, I think you are. You're afraid of what I'm going to bring into your cozy, well-organized life, aren't you, Brenna? With me around you might find yourself tempted to give in to the more adventuresome side of your nature. In fact, the mere act of coming to me takes you very far afield, doesn't it? I keep warning you what giving yourself to me really means, and you keep trying to pretend you can slip in and out of my bed without accepting the commitment it involves. You're frightened of that commitment because it's got nothing to do with your neat little academic world. You're frightened of *me* because I'm not a man from your world. But you've got the courage to handle those fears, Brenna."

"I came here tonight to apologize," Brenna hissed angrily, "not to become involved in this kind of crazy argument! Good night, Ryder." She waited defiantly for him to release his grip on her leg. Not for the world would she admit that she was trembling with an irrational wish that he would simply yank her into the room and into his bed. It made everything so much simpler when she didn't have to make the choice.

"Good night, Brenna. Your apology is accepted." Ryder took his hand away from her thigh. He didn't move as she scrambled back out of the window and fled toward her cabin. But he called her name once softly in the darkness and she halted, poised warily in the starlight. "Brenna."

"Yes, Ryder?"

"You could have kept him here, you know."

"Craig?" She frowned uncertainly, not understanding.

"All you had to do was tell him about your own messy situation at the college. If you'd told him how bad things are and told him you needed his support, he would have stuck around until everything was resolved."

"That wouldn't have been a fair tactic to use," she protested instantly. "It would have been a kind of emotional blackmail."

"I know." She sensed his smile even though she couldn't quite discern it. "And you're a woman of honor, aren't you? You prefer to fight fair, even when you know you're going to lose. Good night, lady. Sleep well."

Nine

It was Ryder who found the note in the mailbox shared by the two cabins. He walked into Brenna's kitchen the next morning just as she was about to poach an egg for herself. He didn't bother to knock.

"It's addressed to you," he announced, tossing the envelope down on the table and lowering himself casually into one of the chairs. "Tea ready yet?"

Brenna refrained from dropping the egg into the swirling hot water and frowned. She had spent a sleepless night alternating between anger and cool determination. Ryder looked as if he'd had a thoroughly restful night. She wanted to say something firm about the way he had walked in without bothering to knock, but she couldn't think of anything that wouldn't sound childish or petulant.

"It's ready. Help yourself." Wiping her hands on a towel, she went over to the table and picked up the small letter. It was from Diana Bergen.

"Friend of yours?" Ryder asked easily, pouring his tea.

"She's a member of the philosophy department. A colleague. Yes, she's a friend." Brenna tore open the envelope and quickly scanned the contents. "So," she whispered when she'd finished. "That's the way it's going to end."

"The way what's going to end?" Ryder persisted patiently, his gaze going to the letter.

Brenna looked up. "She says Dr. Humphrey is announcing his retirement unexpectedly early. There's going to be a party for him tomorrow night and she suggests I come back for it. Good politics." Her mouth turned downward derisively at that last comment. "Says she would have phoned to give me more advance notice but found out I didn't have a telephone here this summer." Brenna glanced back down at the letter. "She also says Damon will undoubtedly be taking over Humphrey's position."

Ryder sipped cautiously at the hot tea. "The fall term should prove interesting for you," he observed dryly. "Are you really going to go back and work for the man you insulted so openly a few days ago?"

Brenna tapped her fingers restlessly on the table. "I'll worry about Damon later. I might be able to apologize for what happened and make him understand," she said quietly. "It's Humphrey I'm thinking about now. If I don't go to this party for him tomorrow evening I may never see him again. If I'm ever going to do or say anything to his face about what he's done to me, tomorrow night is the time."

Ryder ignored the last part of her statement altogether. "What the hell do you mean you'll worry about Fielding later? I thought you said he could make life very uncomfortable for you this fall.''

"He can.'' She shrugged. "But I don't think he will. He *likes* me, Ryder. He'll understand how upset I was just as I understood why he was trying to talk me into not making a scene with Humphrey. He was only trying to make me see the political side of the question.'' She brushed the remainder of that issue aside. "The important thing right now is whether or not I'm going to confront Humphrey.''

"Can he still jeopardize your career?''

"I doubt it. Not from retirement. I could still come out of a scene looking extremely foolish, though. Damon's right in that regard. I'm just a very junior member of the faculty making some crazy charges against a renowned senior member of the department. But I can't let this pass! My God! I worked months on that ethics paper. Some of those conclusions took me weeks of study and analysis. To see them published by a man I held in such high regard is unbearable. I have to say *something* to him, even if I do come off looking foolish and vicious.'' Brenna got to her feet with determination. "I'm going to that party. I'll drive back this afternoon and have plenty of time to prepare for tomorrow night.'' The moment of decision had really arrived and she knew what had to be done. She had to confront Paul Humphrey regardless of what he might do to her future in the academic world. It was a relief to have the decision made.

"What about Fielding?'' Ryder asked very softly.

She turned to glance at him as she prepared to finish making breakfast. "It was wrong of me to expect Damon to help me fight my battles. I shouldn't have tried to enlist his aid, and I had no right to insult him when he tried to make me see his side of the matter. I'll apologize to him tomorrow night. He'll understand why I acted as I did. I'll explain to him about you, too.''

''That should be interesting.''

Brenna felt herself flush furiously and her mouth tightened. ''There's no need for him to know all the details!''

''He's already guessed most of the pertinent ones, as I recall. He thinks I'm the stud you're amusing yourself with this summer, remember?''

''Don't say things like that!'' she whispered tautly, shocked.

''You heard him. Is that how you see me, Brenna?''

''Ryder, don't be ridiculous. You're just trying to provoke me.'' She looked at him pleadingly, the bowl of eggs in her hand. ''Ryder, about last night, I hope you understood what I was trying to say.''

''You have the most annoying tendency to try to explain 'last nights.''' Ryder's crooked smile expressed a tenderness that took Brenna by surprise. She stood quite still, staring at him as he got up from the table and came across the floor to cup her face in his hands. ''But it's the future I'm concerned about. I won't try to tell you that you shouldn't go back for this party. If you feel you have to confront Humphrey, that's your business. It's a matter of pride and honor. I understand that. But I have to know whether or not you're planning on coming back here to Tahoe afterward.''

Brenna went still, her inner turmoil clear in the amber of her eyes. "Ryder, I don't know if I should. Perhaps this is as good a time to end things as any."

"You won't be ending matters if you stay down in the Bay area," he warned gently. "You'll just make it necessary for me to come after you. I'm asking for your word that you'll come back here instead of going into hiding. I think you've got the courage to return, lady. What do you think?" His thumbs moved sensually along the line of her throat, and the silver in his gaze was a net she couldn't avoid.

"Oh, Ryder," she whispered helplessly.

"Your word you'll come back?" he coaxed softly.

What could she say? How could she resist, even though she knew she should? This man might be all wrong for her, but he held a power over her that no other man had ever wielded.

"Ryder, it would be better if—"

He didn't let her finish. Still holding her face cupped in his rough yet gentle hands, he brought his mouth down to take hers in a sweet, lingering kiss that flooded her with weakness and reminded her all too keenly of how close she was to falling in love with Ryder Sterne.

His tongue moved knowingly along the inside of her lips as he deepened the kiss. When she moaned softly and unconsciously crowded a little closer to his hard frame, he lifted his head to look down into her eyes. "Promise you'll come back to Tahoe. You owe me that much at least, lady."

She didn't owe him anything, Brenna told herself wildly even as she heard her own voice say "Yes."

He pulled her close against his chest. "It's always

nice to know one is dealing with a woman who will honor her word.''

Brenna was on her way by lunchtime. She was tense, both from the strain of what she was going to do when she met Paul Humphrey face to face and from the look in Ryder's eyes as he watched her leave. He stood in the drive, feet slightly braced and hands shoved idly into his back pockets. The breeze ruffled his tawny hair and the sun seemed to glance along the planes of his set features. He understood why she had to go, Brenna knew. But he would hold her to her word about returning.

What had she done by rashly giving her promise on that score? she asked herself time and again on the long drive back to the San Francisco Bay area. It would have been so much more rational to simply not have returned. Going back to Tahoe would be dangerous. There was no way around that.

No, she had to stop thinking about such matters. Her main concern now must be deciding what she would say to the esteemed Dr. Humphrey. Brenna entertained no illusions about gaining any real justice out of the mess. But it had become important to let the man know she was well aware of what he had done and what she thought of him for doing it. She was the only one who could stand up for her own rights. It had been wrong to hope that Damon would stand beside her. Some things a person had to do for herself. If there was ever a philosophical bit of truth, that was it!

The apartment she had left for the summer seemed almost unwilling to welcome her back so soon. It was closed up and too neat, just as she had left it. There was also no food in the place.

Hours later, tired by the drive and her own nervous tension, Brenna crawled between the cold sheets, turned on her electric blanket, and fell asleep. And dreamed of a man with silver-gray eyes.

She chose her clothes with care the following evening, the kind of clothes that a woman would wear when she knew she would be standing alone. She wasn't about to fade into the room on this particular occasion. The suit was classic white, spare and cleanly designed with a rakish shape to the upstanding collar that framed her throat. Underneath she wore a chrome-yellow silk blouse. The contrast with her dark hair and the yellow-heeled white leather pumps made an impact that would not go unnoticed. Standing in front of her bedroom mirror, she twisted her hair into a sleek, severe knot and added a yellow and turquoise bracelet to one wrist. The amber in her eyes seemed almost gold as she stared critically back at herself. Would anyone else notice the tension and, yes, the fear in those eyes?

Deliberately choosing to arrive late at the on-campus faculty club, Brenna walked through the quiet grounds with a firm stride that belied her inner nervousness. The college was operating some special summer programs this year, but even with those in progress there wasn't nearly the usual bustle of students and faculty as there was during the academic year.

The understated elegance of the faculty club was the result of a bequest from a generous alumnus. The room had been designed to resemble the gracious library of an English manor house and, as was appropriate, sherry would be the beverage served. Brenna wasn't surprised to see the delicate little tea sandwiches that accompanied it. The staff of the campus cafeteria somehow always managed to produce fairly interesting tidbits for these occasions.

The subdued hum of conversation was as appropriate as the little sandwiches and the sherry. The room was full of faculty members from all of the college's various department, including the library. Brenna stood silently in the doorway for a moment absorbing the scene. Dr. Paul Humphrey was, naturally, the focus of attention of the most important of the evening's guests. The provost and his wife, the head of the library, and several other notables stood grouped around the retiring faculty member. At Humphrey's right hand stood Damon Fielding.

"Brenna! You made it! I'm so glad you got my note."

Diana Bergen came quickly toward her, her attractive features cheerfully drawn into a smile of welcome. She was a couple of years older than Brenna and had recently been promoted to associate professor in the philosophy department.

"Thanks for thinking of me when you heard the news, Diana." Brenna accepted the delicate glass of sherry and took a sip. She was going to need it.

"I really thought it would be a good idea for you to show up." Diana nodded, glancing over her shoulder at the group surrounding Paul Humphrey. "I know Humphrey is a little pompous and no one's going to be overly sad to see him leave, but it's important to be seen at functions like this. A good opportunity to show the provost you have a proper respect for senior members of the faculty community,'' she added with a knowing little chuckle.

A few weeks ago Brenna wouldn't have thought twice about the little customs, niceties, and command performances demanded of a junior faculty member. A certain amount of socializing was important in any job, and she would be the last to belittle the civilizing factor of good manners. But there was no denying that her view was jaundiced this evening. A glance around the room seemed to show nothing but people playing the subtle political game of climbing the academic ladder. Would any of these people even want to know about what had happened to her? Would they care that she had been Humphrey's victim, or would they just as soon never hear about it? She guessed the latter. Once they knew about it, they would have to take sides, and the only sensible side to take was Humphrey's. Humphrey, of course, would deny the whole incident.

She didn't have the right to involve anyone else, anyway, Brenna reminded herself as she circulated quietly through the crowd. This was between herself and Paul Humphrey. She glanced again at his aristocratic profile as he held court in the center of the elegant Oriental carpet. He was a tall man, his thick mane of snow-white hair lending him a patrician air. Somehow she was going to have to manage to get him off by himself.

As she watched him through coolly narrowed eyes, sipping at her sherry, Damon Fielding glanced across the room and saw her. She saw the surprise and dismay in his eyes, and then he was moving toward her.

"Brenna!" He sounded wary. "I'm glad you decided to come tonight. It's about time you realized the facts of academic life. As you can see, Humphrey is virtually out the door. You won't have to work for him in the fall. No point in making a scene now, is there? It was an unpleasant incident but not one worth ruining your image with the rest of the faculty and the provost. I guarantee things will be different when I take over Humphrey's position!"

"Is it settled then? You'll be appointed head?" she queried.

"It's definite. In fact, Humphrey decided to bow out early just so that I could take over a little sooner than planned." There was no hiding the satisfaction in him and he proved it with his next words. "I also want you to know I'm not holding a grudge about what happened in Tahoe, Brenna. I realize you were under a great deal of strain at the time."

"Thank you, Damon," Brenna said slowly, surprised at the magnanimousness of the statement. It gave her the opening to make her own apology and she seized it quickly. "I was so shocked when my neighbor struck you. He overreacted, of course, but you must see how it happened," she added earnestly. "He saw us arguing and he had no way of knowing at the time who you were."

Damon's mouth twisted ruefully and his handsome face seemed to soften with genuine understanding. "I should never have slapped you. That was really all he had a chance to see, and he reacted to it without stopping to ask questions first, didn't he?"

"Something like that, I'm afraid. I'm—I'm sorry

I provoked you, Damon. I had no right to say the things I did. No right at all.''

"Brenna, who was he?'' Damon demanded with an underlying urgency.

"My neighbor.'' Her eyes flickered briefly across the room to track Humphrey's movements.

"Someone important to you?'' Damon persisted. "I was angry at the time and implied a few things I had no right to imply.''

"He's my neighbor for the summer, Damon. A friend.'' How could she possibly begin to explain Ryder Sterne's role in her life when she hadn't figured it out herself?

"I see. Did you tell him about us?'' Damon sounded almost cautious now. "Did you explain why we were arguing that morning? Who I am?''

"I told him who you are,'' Brenna admitted slowly.

"Good,'' he murmured, apparently relieved. "Then he knows what the situation between you and me is.''

Brenna looked at him, thinking how she had intended to try to explain Ryder to Damon. She knew now that would be a pointless effort because she didn't have all the right words to attempt such an explanation. In any event there really wasn't time. She was here on another mission altogether this evening, one Damon seemed to have all too quickly misconstrued. Brenna took a deep breath.

"Damon, I came here tonight because I'm going to confront Humphrey.''

His expression of satisfaction faded into one that,

if she hadn't known better, Brenna might have taken for fear.

"You can't! What would be the point? For God's sake, he's literally out the door! What good can it do you to confront him tonight? Let it be, Brenna, just let it be, will you? You'll only be doing yourself an incredible amount of damage!"

"I just want him to know I'm aware of what he did to me, Damon," she said steadily. "Don't worry, I won't ask you to get involved or take sides. I should never have done that in the first place. This is strictly between Humphrey and myself." She smiled a little grimly. "If it makes you feel any better, rest assured I'm not even going to cause a major scene. That's not my way. I'm not going to stand here and yell at him at the top of my lungs. That would be a—a form of violence, wouldn't it? I'm really not a very violent person. I'm going to take him quietly aside and confront him with what he did. I just want him to know that I know and I want him to be aware of what I think of him. That's all the revenge I'm seeking, Damon, believe me."

"He could still hurt your career, Brenna."

"From out of retirement?"

"Going into retirement doesn't mean he'll be giving up all his associations and his friendships, damn it! He could still put a word or two in certain ears and influence certain people against you!" he argued urgently.

"I'll have to take the risk, Damon. I want to be sure he knows what I think about him for lowering the honor of his profession to this extent."

"Honor!" Damon exploded vengefully. "What

the hell does honor have to do with a career? Brenna, compromises have to be made in every line of work. Let this matter go and your own career can only benefit. It will be worth it to your future to be rational about this!''

She looked at him levelly. ''You mean because I won't be running the risk of Humphrey trying to damage my career?''

''I mean,'' he declared with emphasis, ''that if you'll let things ride, I will personally make it worth your while.'' He returned her astonished expression with one of cool defiance.

''What on earth...? Damon, what are you saying?''

''I'm going to be the new department head, Brenna.''

''Yes, I understand that, but...''

''And as such I will be in a position to, shall we say, *compensate* you for what the outgoing department head did to you.'' He waited, watching her narrowly, the way Brenna imagined a high-powered chief of a large corporation might watch a junior manager to whom he had just offered something akin to a bribe.

''Compensate me,'' she echoed flatly.

''As head of the philosophy department I will have a lot of influence over matters such as promotion and tenure and even publication. You'll find it will be worth your while not to take any step tonight that will jeopardize your career.''

''Damon, are you trying to bribe me?'' she whispered in mingled astonishment and dismay. She couldn't quite believe what she was hearing.

"I can't seem to talk sense into you," he bit out angrily. "And I care too much about you to let you ruin your future. If bribing you to keep silent is what it takes to make you act reasonably this evening, then that's what I'm doing, yes!"

"Oh, Damon," she murmured with a sad little shake of her head. "You just don't understand, and I honestly don't know how to explain any further." But Ryder understood, Brenna thought fleetingly. Ryder comprehended matters of personal justice and honor and ethics even though he'd never made a formal study of them. How could Damon, who *had* made a formal study of them, be so blind? "I appreciate your intentions but I can't let the matter drop. I feel I have to say something to Humphrey. I wonder how many times he's published other people's work as his own?"

"You're going to go through with this act of stupidity even though nothing you say or do will change the situation? Brenna, listen to me!"

But it was too late for further remonstrations on Damon's part. Even as he opened his mouth to continue the argument, a well-modulated masculine voice was breaking in on his words. "Ah, there you are, Fielding. Wondered where you'd gone. Should have guessed when I saw our charming Miss Llewellyn in the crowd, though! So glad to see you again, Brenna, my dear." Paul Humphrey inclined his head with an Old World grace. "Very thoughtful of you to come back for this little farewell the faculty arranged for me. I understood you were spending the summer in Tahoe?"

So charming, so aristocratic and courtly. So esteemed in his profession. Brenna found herself at a loss to understand how this man could look her in the eye and try to charm her as if nothing had happened. She was aware of a thrill of apprehension. Even when you knew you were right, it wasn't always easy to face this kind of scene, she thought. Brenna met the benign gaze with determination.

"I wouldn't have missed this for the world, Dr. Humphrey." Her adrenaline switched into high gear. She would never have a better opportunity. There was only Damon to witness the confrontation, and that didn't really matter since he knew the facts. If he chose to hang around while she faced Paul Humphrey with her accusations, that was his business, but Brenna wondered why he didn't decide to drift off and leave her to her fate. "You see, there was something I wanted to discuss with you before you retired."

Paul Humphrey smiled charmingly. "You needn't worry about my disappearing entirely, my dear. I fully intend to take advantage of all the privileges belonging to retired faculty members. I expect you'll see me around—I understand I'm even going to be allowed to maintain an office in the north wing of the library. Just an old war horse, I'm afraid. I wouldn't be able to stay totally out of harness. But I am going to take a vacation before I adjust to my new role in life. A trip to Greece that my wife and I have been promising ourselves for years," he confided jovially.

"Dr. Humphrey, I really must speak to you," Brenna began formally, her stomach twisting into a knot of tension. This was ridiculous. She must stand up for her rights. She must let this man know what she thought of him. She owed it to herself and to the honor of her profession.

"Of course, my dear." He winked broadly. "But I'll bet I can guess what it is you want to discuss!"

Brenna parted her lips to begin the quiet accusation, but before she could get the first words out of her mouth she became aware of two things almost simultaneously.

The first was the utterly beseeching expression on Damon Fielding's face. He was silently pleading with her not to continue. *Does he really care that much about my future career?* she wondered, taken aback.

The second factor that impinged on her consciousness at that crucial juncture was a faint sensation of heightened awareness. It was the kind of sensation that made you turn your head in a crowd and look around to see who was watching you.

For a split second Brenna succumbed to the primitive pull and slid a quick, uneasy glance toward the door. She turned her head just in time to see Ryder enter the room.

For an instant she couldn't move, quite stunned by his presence. What was Ryder doing there? In the next moment she realized that there could be only one explanation. He hadn't trusted her to return to Tahoe.

The knowledge of that mistrust bit deep. It was suddenly more important than anything else this evening, including her confrontation with Paul Humphrey. *Ryder hadn't trusted her to keep her word!*

Across the room, Ryder's glance collided with

hers. He barely nodded at the polite but curious hostess who was pushing a delicate sherry glass into his hand. His silver eyes never left Brenna's as he started toward her.

It was like watching a jungle cat glide across the room. Ryder had dressed for the occasion, but apparently without any concern for the style of masculine dress favored in the pompous atmosphere of a faculty club. He certainly wasn't wearing anything like the British tweeds or the quiet, conservative suits that predominated in the room. The fawn-colored sportcoat was cut with Continental flair, not British conservatism, and it was shaped out of the supplest of suedes. The slacks were a darker brown, lean-fitting and expensive. The tie was a bold splash of gold and brown and it was worn over a brown silk shirt. With his tawny hair, he resembled a lion to Brenna's stricken gaze.

"I beg your pardon, my dear," Paul Humphrey prompted politely in a bid to regain her attention.

She forced herself to turn back to the task at hand, fiercely aware of the fact that Ryder was almost upon her. She could only tackle one thing at a time, she reminded herself. Ryder's mistrust would have to be dealt with later.

"Brenna, please!" Damon's tight voice broke into her concentration.

"About the paper you're publishing on the subject of computer ethics, Dr. Humphrey," she began challengingly, feeling as if everything were happening at once and knowing she had to regain control of herself and the situation.

"Ah, yes," Humphrey nodded imperturbably.

"I'm not at all surprised you're interested in it. I hope you'll be able to get something useful out of it for your own project. I understand you're working on a related issue?" One white brow arched in polite inquiry.

Brenna nearly choked on her last sip of sherry. "Get something useful out of it!"

"Brenna, listen to me!"

Damon again. With a flash of insight triggered by the knowledge of Ryder's presence behind her, Brenna realized she was strangely glad that Damon Fielding had chosen not to stand beside her in this matter. For if he had, she would need to feel somewhat obligated to him, and the last thing she wanted now was a feeling of obligation toward Damon. She wanted to be free, totally free, to go to Ryder. The impact of that knowledge was almost overwhelming.

"Yes, indeed," Dr. Humphrey was continuing expansively. "But quite frankly, if it's clarification or amplification you need, I suggest you talk to Dr. Fielding, here."

Brenna looked up at him blankly. Ryder was right at her shoulder now, not speaking or touching her but indisputably *there.* She could feel the power of his presence but she focused her attention completely on Paul Humphrey.

"Dr. Fielding and I held several discussion on the topic before I wrote the paper. He made some extraordinarily insightful comments and suggestions. So many, in fact, that, although he insists he doesn't want any credit, I'm going to see to it that his name goes on that paper as well as my own. No, no, Fielding, don't bother to argue. I believe in giving credit where credit is due, and you know full well I would never have written that paper without your urging and your helpful contributions. It was truly a joint effort, and I'm going to see to it that you receive proper acknowledgment. Some of those conclusions were brilliant, positively brilliant!''

Brenna swung her wide-eyed gaze to Damon. Behind her Ryder sipped sherry, his cool, watchful, prepared attitude registering itself on Brenna's consciousness.

''You contributed *significantly* to Dr. Humphrey's paper?'' she breathed. ''Exactly what contributions did you make, Dr. Fielding? By any chance were the sections on Humanist ethics and twentieth-century logic your work?''

Before a grim and desperate-looking Damon could reply, Dr. Humphrey was again interrupting expansively. ''Oh, yes, Dr. Fielding made a number of points in that area. He also brought in the rather unusual sections on Aristotelian thinking, didn't you, Damon?''

Brenna's fingers gripped the little sherry glass until her knuckles whitened. All of those interpretations and analyses had been hers. All of them!

''And the comments on Kant?'' she pursued relentlessly.

''Brenna, I can explain...''

''If you two will excuse me,'' Humphrey murmured, ''I think I'll let you get on with this discussion. I do have an obligation to circulate this evening.'' He chuckled. ''Have to let everyone show how much they'll miss me!'' He patted Damon paternally on the shoulder and moved off with a curious glance and nod at Ryder.

He wasn't the only one flicking a glance at the silent Ryder. Damon's expression of grim desperation was tightening. Brenna stared at him.

"Damon, how could you?" she whispered fiercely. "You stole my work. You knew those notes were in my desk drawer. It must have been easy for you. And I spent so much time telling you about my project. It must have been simple for you to outline the best portions and feed them to Dr. Humphrey as your own 'contributions.' But why? I don't understand *why.*"

"Brenna, I can explain," Damon began, his eyes still moving nervously from her to Ryder and back. "But this is between you and me. What's *he* doing here? Get rid of him!"

For the first time Ryder spoke, not moving from his position at Brenna's shoulder. His voice was very gentle and, therefore very, very menacing.

"I don't believe in letting my woman handle the bloody work on her own, even though she's got the guts to do it."

"The bloody work!" Damon looked quite dazed.

"She thinks I'm something of a chauvinist, but that's the way it is." Ryder shrugged, downing a swallow of the rich sherry. His cool glance moved meaningfully over Brenna's taut features as she looked up at him and met his eyes directly for the first time since he had entered the room. "Well?" he said blandly. "Is he the one?" He indicated Damon with a casual thumb.

"Apparently so," she got out tightly.

"Brenna, it was a matter of establishing myself firmly enough in Humphrey's mind that he would make an effort to handpick his own successor. Whoever he names will get the nod for department head! Don't you see? In that position I can help both of us!"

"What do you want done with him, lady?" There was a subtle anticipation in Ryder's words that Damon reacted to immediately. He stepped back a pace even though the other man hadn't moved.

"Brenna, this is ridiculous. I can see you're not prepared to listen to reason," Damon sputtered furiously.

"Forget it, Ryder," Brenna murmured icily. "I only came here tonight to tell the guilty party what I thought of his actions. That's already been accomplished, hasn't it, Damon? You surely know what I think of you. Your climb up the academic ladder should be interesting. What will you think of yourself when you get to the top, I wonder?"

Before her colleague could reply, Brenna swung around on a yellow-heeled shoe and put her hand lightly on Ryder's arm. "I'm ready to go now," she told him, lifting her chin proudly. "I've done what I came to do."

"You're satisfied?" he asked, searching her face intently.

"Yes, I'm satisfied. Please get me out of here."

"My pleasure."

Ten

Ryder led her toward the door with an arrogant disregard for the discreetly curious glances they were receiving. Brenna found herself aware of the expressions of her friends and colleagues but in that moment found them fading into unimportance compared with the absolutely critical matter she had to discuss with Ryder. Now that it was behind her, even the scene with Damon was no longer the most vital issue in her world. As soon as the door closed behind them, she glared up at his profile.

"Why did you follow me? I told you I'd come back to Tahoe!"

"I know what you told me, lady," he drawled softly.

"But you didn't believe me, is that it? You thought I'd run? Ryder, I gave you my word!" She came to a decisive halt on the sidewalk and he obediently stopped too, somehow contriving to maneuver her into the light of the streetlamp.

"I know you gave me your word. That's not why I decided to show up tonight," he stated evenly.

"Then why are you here?" she rasped huskily.

"For the reason I gave Fielding, naturally. What else?" He took her arm again and started her along the sidewalk.

"The reason you gave Damon! Oh!" Brenna's lashes closed briefly in sudden comprehension. Then she opened them to slant him a sidelong glance. "You drove all the way down here from Tahoe just to be around in case there was any, uh, 'bloody' work that needed doing?" She found herself remembering how the hero in *The Quicksilver Venture* always stepped in to handle the dirty business so that Cass didn't have to face the danger alone. It had been a manifestation of Hunt Cameron's chauvinism. It had also been a manifestation of his caring.

"Even though you aren't violence-prone"—Ryder broke off to touch the side of his face absently in memory—"or at least not generally prone toward it, I still didn't want you tackling the guy who stole your material by yourself. It's not that I didn't think you could handle it, I just didn't want you doing it alone. I have the right to look after you now, Brenna," he concluded flatly. "I have the right to stand by you when you're facing something serious."

"The right!" Brenna dragged them both to another forcible halt, narrowing her eyes ferociously as she peered up at him. "The *right!* Ryder Sterne, you're a chauvinistic, arrogant male who has presumed far too much, assumed too many rights, made too many claims since we first met, but—'' She had to stop to catch her breath.

''But?'' he repeated, his hands moving slowly up and down her arms. He seemed concerned by her outburst, but utterly determined.

''But at least a woman always knows exactly where she stand with you,'' Brenna admitted frankly. ''And she always knows where you yourself will stand: beside her when she needs you. Thank you for coming tonight, Ryder.'' Impulsively she stood on tiptoe, bracing herself with her hands on his shoulders, and brushed her lips lightly against his firm mouth.

Then she swept on toward the parking lot without giving him a chance to react. He paced silently beside her to where she had parked her car, not speaking until he had opened her door for her.

''I'll wait for you in Tahoe,'' he told her calmly, handing back the keys he had taken long enough to unlock the door. ''Drive carefully tomorrow.''

Brenna paused in the act of slipping into the front seat, confused. ''You're going back? Tonight?''

''Yes. I only came down in case there were fireworks. That's the truth, lady.'' He smiled warmly into her anxious eyes.

''Not because you didn't trust me to return?''

''I trust you to keep your word.''

She caught her breath at the look in his eyes. ''It's a long drive back,'' she whispered tentatively.

''I'll be all right.''

''You could stay here,'' she pointed out in a little rush.

He shook his head. ''I want you to know I trust you. Drive carefully, lady. I'll be waiting for you tomorrow. Go back to your apartment tonight and get some sleep. You've had a rough evening.'' He shut her car door and stepped back, waiting until she reluctantly started the engine before he walked over to the Ferrari and climbed inside. They went their separate ways as they drove out of the campus parking lot.

She could follow him back tonight, Brenna told herself, watching the Ferrari disappear in the rearview mirror. Why hadn't he encouraged her to do exactly that? Because he knew she needed some time by herself in which to think? He was a very perceptive man. She *did* need time to think. A lot of the problems she'd been struggling with had resolved themselves this evening: her future in the academic world, her knowledge of what she wanted out of life, and her acceptance of her relationship with Ryder. Yes, she needed time to think, not to come to conclusions but to adjust to the conclusions that had made themselves plain tonight. It was like studying philosophy, she thought as she drove back to her apartment. You could go over and over a complex bit of logic without understanding it, and then all at once everything fell into place.

For her that falling into place had occurred when she'd looked across the room and seen Ryder walking toward her, asserting his right to be at her side.

He might find the concept of love sloppy and sentimental, Brenna decided the next morning as she repacked the small overnight bag she'd brought with her and locked the apartment again for the summer, but Ruder knew all there was to know about the fundamentals behind the word. More than Damon Fielding would ever know, she added silently to herself as she began the long drive back to Lake Tahoe.

She might disagree with Ryder's way of doing things from time to time, but her respect for him would never be lowered. He was a man who understood the basics of what she had been trying so hard to teach this past semester in Ethics 205. And he'd arrived at that understanding on his own. She wasn't sure where the commitment she was making to him would lead, but she knew for certain that she would be able to trust his commitment to her completely.

The drive back to Tahoe seemed to take forever, but she was on the winding lakeside drive by morning and turning into the lane that led to the cabins shortly thereafter. It was only a summer place but she felt as if she were coming home.

She couldn't explain the wave of shyness that momentarily assailed her as she braked the car to a halt in front of the cabin and saw Ryder coming toward her from behind the house. He set the bow and quiver of arrows he had been using aside on the porch as he came forward. Brenna just looked at him for a long moment, drinking in the sight of him and feeling the sureness of her decision welling up inside her.

When that sureness threatened to block the breath in her throat, she threw open the car door and began to run.

"Ryder, oh my darling, I'm sorry I took so long!" She hurled herself into his waiting arms and he locked them closed around her, swinging her effortlessly around in a circle before letting her find her feet.

"I knew you'd come back," he growled gently, and then he was pinning her close for a slow, savoring kiss that branded and claimed and promised. Time hung suspended for the length of that kiss and Brenna gave herself up to it with willing surrender, for she knew she was staking her own feminine claim. This man was hers.

When he finally lifted his head reluctantly to smile searchingly down into her glowing face, Ryder seemed shaken by the wonder of what her kiss must have told him and by the evident love in her eyes. "Does this mean you're not merely coming back because you've agreed to give our relationship a chance? Have you made your decision, Brenna? Will you be accepting my claim completely?"

She laughed up at him wickedly. "Ryder, you have a way of expressing yourself that badly needs refining for the modern age of equality. I'm here for the sloppy, sentimental reason that I love you. I know," she went on hurriedly, stopping his mouth with her palm when he would have spoken, "you don't think much of the word, but I find it perfect to describe my feelings for you. And someday I'm going to convince you that it's the perfect way to describe your feelings for me," she concluded tenderly.

He kissed the fingers that covered his lips and she lowered them, her cheeks warming at the expression on his face. "I never said I thought the word 'love' was sloppy and sentimental," he whispered. "I said my readers would probably find it so. I avoided using it with you because I figured one had to trap a rational little professor with logic and appeals to her sense of integrity and honor. There's no logic to love.''

''But there is honor and integrity,'' she said.

''Yes.'' He slid his hands into her hair, pulling free the combs that had anchored it back behind her ears. ''Brenna, I love you. I knew I wanted you from the first. It didn't take me long to realize the feeling went much deeper than that. I need you in a way I can't fully explain. You're like the other half of myself. I'm more than willing to label that feeling 'love.'''

''So am I, Ruder. So am I.''

He drew her close to his chest, smoothing the length of her hair and sliding his hands up and down her back with a heavy urgency, as if he still couldn't believe she had accepted him completely.

''We're on the Nevada side of the lake, lady,'' he murmured.

''So?'' She smiled into his shirt, luxuriating in the wonder of being held by him.

''So we can get married this afternoon without any waiting.''

She lifted her head. ''Is that what you want, Ryder?''

''It's what I want. I have a very primitive need to tie you to me with all the bonds I can find.''

She shook her head, her amber eyes smiling at him. ''What am I going to do with you? No sense of what a modern relationship entails at all!''

''Stop making fun of my Neanderthal approach and tell me you'll marry me,'' he ordered roughly, using his hand to pull her head back down onto his shoulder.

"I'll marry you," she agreed obediently.

"If only for the opportunity of straightening out my male chauvinism?"

"I never could resist a challenge."

She felt a tremor of laughter go through him and he kissed the curve of her shoulder. Brenna lifted her arms to wrap them around his neck. "Oh, Ryder, I love you so. I kept telling myself you were all wrong for me but I guess that was because I was afraid of realizing how very *right* you really were."

"In spite of my past? I know I don't have the kind of background you probably expected to find in the man you married…"

"It's not your past I'm interested in." She smiled. "Only your present and your future."

He sighed, a kind of relief evident in the sound. "And your future, Brenna? Do you know what you want now?"

"I know, I want you. As for the rest, I'm open to suggestion," she admitted. "For as long as I can remember I've kept myself on the straight and narrow path of academia. It's a good path and someday I may go back to it. But right now I think I'd like a change. At least for the next few months. I wonder if you would be interested in seeing a little of the world with me? There are some things I've missed during the past few years. Things I'd like to catch up on."

"As a matter of fact," he said gently, "I was thinking of taking a couple of research trips after I finish this current book."

"I should warn you that, unlike Craig, I like my adventure with a few luxuries."

"Oh, it will be first class, all the way." He grinned. "It's the only way I'm interested in traveling now myself!"

"And when we get back I will rethink my career plans. I'm not really sure what I want to do, and it's rather nice thinking that I have the freedom to change everything if I wish. I've never given myself that freedom before."

"Well, since your future is still a little unsettled," Ryder drawled, "would you be interested in hearing some plans for the immediate present?"

"I feel quite open to suggestions."

"Fine. Then this is what we're going to do. First, I will bundle you into the car and whisk you off to the nearest wedding chapel. Then we shall have a light lunch of champagne and caviar and then I shall carry you off to the bedroom where we can celebrate our future in style."

"I love it when you're being masterful," she said, grinning, eyes sparkling.

Three hours later Ryder poured the last of the champagne and saluted his new bride. "To the lady cat burglar who came crawling through my window at two in the morning." He downed the champagne with relish.

"I think you must be running short of toasts to resort to that one," Brenna observed, the gold of her new wedding band catching the afternoon sunlight as she obediently sipped from her glass.

"That's a very important one," he protested, rising to his feet and setting down the glass with a deliberate air. "After all, that was the night I began to realize I was fated to marry a most adventuresome lady. And I was right, wasn't I? Just look how you seduced me the night we went gambling!''

"I didn't seduce you!''

"Our first married argument? How charming.''

"Ryder? Where are you going?'' She watched him disappear into the hall.

"To get a blanket. We're going down to that little cove on the lake where you read *The Quicksilver Venture.*''

"We are? I thought you were going to carry me off to the bedroom.''

"I've changed my mind. A captured lady cat burglar needs something a little more exciting on her wedding day.''

Brenna laughed softly. "So we're going fishing, instead?''

"Not quite.''

He led her down to the private cove and spread the blanket out with aplomb. Brenna watched him lovingly, enjoying the grace in his body and the sureness of his movements. But when he straightened and turned to look at her, she wasn't prepared for the sudden hesitancy in his silver eyes.

"Ryder?'' she whispered, not understanding.

"Brenna, I love you, and now that you're mine, now that you've finally accepted my claim, I find I'm suffering an attack of groom's jitters. See?'' He held out his hand and there was, indeed, a faint trembling.

Brenna stared at his hand and then her gaze flew to his shimmering eyes. "Are you jittery because you think you may have made a mistake in marrying me?'' The words almost stuck in her throat.

"No! Damn it, don't say such things. That's not it at all!" He closed the distance between them in one gliding stride and hauled her into his arms. "My God, woman, how can you even say that? I'm shaking like a leaf because nothing has ever been as important to me as you are. I want to be the perfect husband, the perfect lover. I want you to love me for the rest of our lives. When you want something that much, you get a little shaky!"

"Maybe that's why I'm trembling, too," she confessed, collapsing against him in the relief of knowing she wasn't the only one who was suffering from bridal jitters. "I want to be the perfect wife for you."

"Lady, lady," he crooned gently, his hands moving on her back, sliding down to her waist.

She lifted her mouth to his and he took her lips with an urgent longing that spoke of want and need and love. They held each other until the case of nerves had subsided. It was a silent time of tenderness and passion that somehow set the seal on the wedding vows they had taken earlier that day.

When Brenna felt the heat rising in Ryder's body, she crowded closer to him and her nails slipped delicately down his back.

"I love you, Ryder."

"My sweet Brenna, I love you so much!" He sank down onto the blanket, pulling her to him in a rush of emotion that could not be halted now that it had begun. With hands that trembled now from passion rather than nerves, he undressed her, fumbling occasionally and cursing a little at his own unaccustomed clumsiness.

The muffled words made Brenna laugh tenderly

and she captured his hands to still them for a moment when he would have unzipped her jeans. ''Wait, you're getting ahead of me!''

He raised his head from where he had buried his lips in her throat and looked down at her questioningly.

''It's only fair to let me fumble a little, too,'' she whispered, releasing his hands and putting her fingers to the buttons of his shirt.

''I suppose we'll get slicker at this as we gain experience,'' he murmured ruefully.

''I suppose.''

''On the other hand I may never get used to the idea of really having you all to myself!'' With that he went back to sliding off the jeans and pushing aside the edges of her shirt.

When they both lay naked at last, Ryder slipped his hands roughly, passionately along the length of rounded thigh and up to the softness of her breasts. The possessiveness in him was a tangible force.

''Oh, Ryder, my love!'' Her voice was a soft moan of wonder and love that he responded to with a flaring desire. She thrilled to the touch of his tongue curling around each nipple, coaxing it tautly awake. His leg moved over hers, forcing her thighs gently apart so that the hand he was trailing across the satin of her stomach could begin teasing the tangled thicket between her legs.

She shifted languidly beneath his exploring, probing touch, her body caught up in the sweet passion being generated between them. Eyes closed tightly in mounting ecstasy, she trailed her fingertips across the crisp hair of his chest, blindly seeking the flat, male nipples. When he groaned she moved, sinking her teeth lightly around the area she had just been caressing.

"Lady witch," he breathed and slipped his hand through the thicket to the dampening heart of her desire. "You open for me like a flower. A hot, luscious passion flower."

"Ryder!" His name was a husky cry on her lips as he boldly stroked the petals of the flower. He leaned close to drink the sound of her moan from the other blossom that was her mouth.

Brenna felt entranced, enthralled, and overwhelmed with the hard strength of him, and she ran her hands again and again across the contours of his back and the muscled power of his thighs. When she trailed them lingeringly, daringly to the point where the tapering chest hair became enmeshed with the provocative curls below his waist, he moved against her. Deliberately he pressed his hardness against her.

"Touch me, lady!" he half commanded, half pleaded. "I love the feel of your soft hands."

But when she willingly did as he asked, his body seemed to surge against her fingers, seeking far more than the caress of her hand. He lifted himself and came down along the length of her body, using his ankles to open her legs farther for his advance. She was ready for him.

"I want you," he grated. And then he was thrusting himself forward against her softness, losing himself in her body even as he mastered it.

Brenna gasped at the delicious impact of him, knowing it would always be thus between them, a kind of mastery and a kind of surrender that blended so that it would be impossible in the ultimate moment to know where the boundaries were or which of them was responsible for which emotion.

He seemed to relinquish all control, giving himself completely even as he took. Brenna clung tightly, her nails raking his back in the heat of her aching need. When he slid one hand down to her buttocks to lift her even more tightly against him, she cried out with husky fierceness and clutched him with a sweet savagery that seemed to call to his most elemental maleness.

His body surged hungrily into hers again and again, sweeping her with him into a taut, whirling vortex from which there was only one exit point.

Brenna let herself go as he flashed with her toward that ending. It was an incredibly exhilarating sensation to know that she could abandon herself to Ryder's embrace, emotionally, physically, even intellectually. They belong to each other.

The tight, spiraling ecstasy within her snapped with unexpected fury and she heard herself calling his name as if it were a talisman.

"Ryder!"

"Yes, sweet lady, *yes!*"

Her body went into a shivering delight, and the tiny convulsions seemed to be more than his own hardness could resist. In an instant he was sinking his fingers deep into the skin of her shoulders, arching himself against her with a near-voiceless shout of triumph and satisfaction. Brenna held him to her with all the passion and love in her heart.

Slowly, lingeringly, they surfaced, still wrapped tightly together. In a tangle of perspiration-dampened arms and legs they let themselves float back to the real world and the privacy of the cove. Lovingly Brenna pressed her lips to his throat, inhaling the scent of their lovemaking as it combined with the mountain breeze. Ryder's fingers moved with tender idleness along her arm and she felt him smile into her hair.

"My wife," he murmured in tones of gentle wonder. "My God, I waited a long time for you to walk into my life!"

"You've been looking for a wife for a long time?" she teased.

"No. Didn't even realize I wanted one until you came sneaking through my window that night. But once I realized that, I knew I'd been waiting for quite a while."

"I was not sneaking!"

"Scared the daylights out of me," he protested.

"Ah, well, it probably served you right," she decided. "I don't think you've had much opportunity to experience being scared."

"Oh, I've been scared a lot since that night," he vowed gently. "Scared Damon Fielding might lure you back, scared you wouldn't be able to tolerate my past, scared you'd try to run from me after I'd made you mine."

"You overwhelm me," she breathed. "I had no idea. But I've been a little scared myself."

"You've had a hell of a lot to deal with these past few days, haven't you? The crisis in your career, Craig's announcement that he wasn't going back to the university…"

"And you. Above all else there was you to deal

with, Ryder Sterne,'' she concluded, rising on one elbow to gaze down at him. ''You were the most complicated thing of all to deal with and you must know that.''

''Because I wasn't what you'd always admired and wanted in a man?''

''No, because you were exactly what I'd always admired and wanted in a man but you didn't come packaged quite the way I had expected you to be packaged. No tweed jacket, no year at Oxford, no Ph.D., no academic credits.''

''Wait a minute,'' he broke in grinning. ''I *have* been published!''

''You've got a point there. Of course, it wasn't quite the sort of publishing I had expected my future husband to be doing,'' she agreed thoughtfully.

''The pay is good,'' he pointed out hopefully.

She giggled. ''And, damn it, the writing is good, too!''

''You liked the story?'' He slid her a speculative glance.

''I loved the story. Except for the violent parts. The love scenes were terrific.''

''Sex scenes,'' he corrected. ''I don't write love scenes.''

''Anybody as good as you are at doing love scenes for real can't help but write them beautifully!'' she proclaimed grandly.

He groaned and pulled her down, trapping her head close by locking his hand around the back of her neck. His other hand traced the outline of her breast lovingly, finding the nipple and coaxing it forth. Ryder's mouth found hers in a kiss of recent satisfaction that combined with a promise of future need. Gently his tongue pried apart her willing lips and he tasted deeply for a long moment of the warmth behind them. With slow reluctance he released her mouth.

"So you want to do a little adventuring before you decide whether or not to go back to the academic world, hmmm?"

"Being with you will be an adventure in itself," she said, smiling, knowing it was the truth.

"You won't mind being married to a macho writer of sleazy men's fiction?" The silver eyes were gleaming with laughter but Brenna chose to take the question seriously.

"I don't mind being married to a man who lives by a code of honor, a man who will always stand beside me when the going gets rough, a man who knows how to love even if he'd never allow the word into one of his sleazy novels!"

"Is that how you see me?" he asked wonderingly.

"Yes," she admitted simply. "You know more about honor and ethics than any of my colleagues seem to know. The advantages of being a self-taught man, I guess."

"Some of that learning came at a high price, Brenna," he warned.

"The price, whatever it was, has been paid. It's over. We are concerned only with our future," she declared, leaning close for an instant to brush his lips with her own.

He smiled at her silver eyes full of love. "Speaking of the future reminds me that I have a piece of sleazy men's fiction to write in the next few weeks.

I'd best get started on it right away so that we can have the rest of the summer to go adventuring. Come here.'' He caught her tenderly and brought her down into a sensuous sprawl on his chest. ''I want to practice my love scenes.''

''I thought you only wrote sex scenes!''

''I think they're definitely going to be love scenes from now on!'' He captured her mouth once more with his own and she realized he had spoken the truth.

Ryder Sterne did love scenes perfectly.

*   *   *   *   *

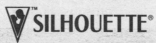